KV-414-682

WINGS OF DESTINY

Joseph Linnett sells his printing business in London and takes his family on a sailing ship bound for Australia. Unfortunately the ship hits the doldrums and is becalmed for two and a half months. Beth, the eldest of Joseph's children, finds romance on the voyage. Joanna, the tomboy of the family, is quite happy to emigrate but fails to realise that Freddie, their neighbour's son, loves her dearly — but who is the stranger in her life?

Books by Barbara Best
in the Linford Romance Library:

THE HOUND OF TRURAN

BARBARA BEST

WINGS
OF
DESTINY

□□
Oldham □□□□ **Libraries**

AL   A2 974 554 X

Classification

LINFORD
Leicester

First Linford Edition
published July 1995

All rights reserved

British Library CIP Data

Best, Barbara
    Wings of destiny.—Large print ed.—
Linford romance library
I. Title II. Series
823. [F]

    ISBN 0–7089–7737–5

Published by
F. A. Thorpe (Publishing) Ltd.
Anstey, Leicestershire

Set by Words & Graphics Ltd.
Anstey, Leicestershire
Printed and bound in Great Britain by
T. J. Press (Padstow) Ltd., Padstow, Cornwall

This book is printed on acid-free paper

1

"TAKE 'em, Fick. I'll walk home. Don't know how long I'll be," said Mr. Frederick Martin.

The tall young man flung this order at his groom and sprang lightly down from a beautifully balanced light brown sporting vehicle. A long cream driving coat enveloped his well developed figure fanning out behind him as he moved swiftly to the front door of Jade Place, the residence of Mr. and Mrs. Joseph Linnett.

The house, named long ago by some forgotten Nabob who had made his fortune trading in exotic carvings from the East, was solidly built in the style of Elizabeth I's era to commemorate her name and ranked as one of the first in style and elegance.

Appearances, however, were deceptive.

The butler had already opened the door and was standing under the semi-circular fanlight with its jewelled coloured glass. He ushered Mr. Martin into an impressive hall which had a wide, elegant stairway that branched away at the top.

"Good afternoon to you, Master Freddie. I hope to see you well?" His rheumy eyes were a little bewildered and his white hair inching from his baldpate made Freddie suddenly conscious that he had known this old man all his life, and who had saved him from many a youthful escapade.

"No need to stand on ceremony with me Swales, old fellow. I'll see myself up. Girls in the old schoolroom? Hmm?" divesting himself of his coat and gloves and without waiting for an answer ran up the stairs two at a time.

"Indeed yes, Master Freddie," murmured the old man still with that look of perplexity as he watched Freddie disappear. He shook his head and went in search of his wife in the kitchen regions, where she was busy preparing the dinner with the help of the tweeny with the most unlikely name of Esmeralda.

Mr. Swales sat down heavily in a chair next to the stove.

"My dearie," exclaimed his wife. "What's wrong? Here, I'll make you a cup of tea with a drop of brandy in it. You do look poorly," with an anxious frown on her pleasant, round face topped by a mob-cap.

"Annie? Is Master Freddie one of ours? For a horrible moment out there I — I couldn't remember."

Relief flooded Mrs. Swales. She laughed. "Well, now don't you go thinking you're all about in your head, my dearie, seeing as how the children of both Mr. Linnett and Squire Martin lived right next door with never a hedge or wall between have been coming and going through this house for the last twenty-six years. You can't be blamed for not remembering one

3

from t'other, now can you, Mr. Swales, dearie?"

"You too, Annie?" her spouse quavered with a sudden lightening of his lined countenance.

"Well," hedged Mrs. Swales with a considering look, hands on hips. "I've done as Madam and Mrs. Martin has done, bless 'em. Just as long as each chair in their dining-rooms for meals, each has a little body, both mothers is satisfied. That way no one is missing, see, but — " shaking her mob-cap with something like despair. "I haven't been able to know whose clothes are whose." She chuckled fatly. "But there was that time, I well remember, when a new maid set one too many chairs at Mrs. Martin's table. Well, what a to do! Remember, dearie?"

Mr. Swales nodded, pleased that he could recall that incident.

"Everyone out hunting for a little 'un. Ha! And only after some time did someone think to count the chairs. Easier done than gathering

4

all those little dears together," he chortled gleefully slapping a hand on to his trousered leg.

* * *

The schoolroom upstairs in Jade Place was a cosy room exuding a genteel air of shabbiness. It was one of the smaller apartments and in it were seated three young ladies all swathed in spencers and shawls against the very cold day in March.

"Oh dear," sighed Lizzie, the youngest daughter of Mr. and Mrs. Linnett. "Why can't the sun shine?" huddling her stout little body more closely in its coverings. "We never have good fires anymore, and I do wish something exciting would happen," she grizzled fretfully.

"There's no money to buy extra coals. Mother said so," retorted Joanna. "And stop pressing your nose against the windowpane. It'll be quite crooked by the time you are a young lady."

Lizzie hunched a pettish shoulder. "I don't care."

"Don't care was made to care, don't care was hung, don't care was put in a pot and boiled until it was done," intoned Joanna, turning back to Miss Austin's *Pride and Prejudice*. She had read it several times but the story continued to fascinate her. The deep blue of her eyes, so richly lashed, matched her simple cotton dress, with its attendant white collar.

Joanna was the tomboy of the family and at just eighteen was the despair of her mother who thought it high time that her daughter's behaviour should become a little more circumspect. Her honeybrown hair was always untidy but her father would not have it so. He liked the beguiling twinkle which shone beneath that, often, untidy fringe.

"Now now, Eliza," he would say to his wife, "Jodear is as sound as a roast. You know that, so why worry?"

Beth, sixteen months older, was the complete opposite with a generous

6

nature and an endearing manner, quite content to let the world pass by, except in the matter of Bertie. She was a quiet person rather than shy, her face with its delicate bone structure and expressive hazel eyes reflecting her every mood.

She was busy sewing buttons on to a shirt for Jed, which she had just finished making.

"Lizzie, you could help me by sewing on some buttons to Jed's other shirt," she suggested quietly, "or mend those stockings of yours. They are piling up in that workbasket." But these suggestions failed to meet Lizzie's taste.

"What I want to know is, why are we so poor?" she asked. "It was never like this before."

"Something to do with the Industrial Revolution," replied Joanna. "The workers don't like the new machinery in the manufactories."

"So?" asked Lizzie.

"Don't you remember that our workers smashed Father's new machinery? That is why money is short," supplied Beth, nibbling off a thread. "Mother told me that Father had paid a lot of money for that machinery from America."

"Birth pangs of the age," murmured Joanna vaguely, her eyes still on her book. "Workers rebelling. It's been going on for years."

Lizzie still at the window said suddenly. "There's a curricle drawing up. Wonder who it can be?" Animation tinged her tones.

"It cannot be for us. We don't entertain any more," said Joanna.

"It's only Freddie," said Lizzie lapsing again into listlessness.

Freddie entered unceremoniously and sat down astride one of the less rickety chairs. He had known these three young ladies all their lives, so niceties were not observed.

"You're fine as fivepence, Freddie," said Joanna, openly admiring the superb cut of his russet coat and fawn trousers accompanied by a pale yellow waistcoat.

"You are improving, Jodear, to have

at last noticed what I am wearing."

She acknowledged the hit with a wide friendly grin which caused Freddie to chuckle.

"Been to town for m'father. Some business about the Home Farm."

"Oh! Not on the strut, dear Sir?"

"No, Jodear." His warm grey eyes, below the thatch of dark hair, twinkled responsively to her teasing.

Joanna knew that he would have been more comfortable in less formal wear, striding over his father's fields with a dog at his heels, his hair tousled by the wind or the rain. Indeed, although his face was boyish, his complexion spoke of time spent out in the open. He was not handsome in the strictest sense of the word but his features were pleasant and his smile was warm.

To Joanna he was just another brother, a far kinder one than Douglas who was now married to the dearest girl and living in a tiny house not far from Jade Place.

Freddie was looking at Beth a little anxiously.

"Bethie, what's wrong? You haven't said a word since I came in. That poor shirt has been stared out of all countenance. It's Bertie, isn't it?"

The Martins and Linnetts were so close that nothing ever was hidden that concerned any of them.

Beth, her fair head lowered to hide the telltale blush, nodded mutely.

"I would like to see him once more to say goodbye." Her voice wobbled with the effort to hide her feelings.

"Uncle Joseph has forbidden you to see him again?"

Another nod and a barely suppressed sob. "He — he wants to marry me."

"Bertie as a man is a very pleasant person but he'd make a very bad husband, Bethie," replied Freddie, wishing they were children again and he could comfort this little friend of his in a more effective manner. Many had been the times he'd lent a shoulder on which to lean when Jodear or Beth had been in trouble. They now were grown up and one had to preserve the conventions in that respect.

"I believe Bertie's the despair of his parents," said Joanna sadly. "I think he gambles money away as fast as he breathes."

Beth protested at this. "Bertie truly loves me. He certainly would not be marrying me for my money. I have no expectations."

"But Bethie, dear," Joanna went on. "He has never done anything in his life except lounge in the most expensive clubs and is thoroughly lazy. No wonder Father won't consider him as a suitable husband for you," and wished the words unsaid as she saw the pain she had caused this much loved sister of hers. "Oh, Bethie, I'm sorry. This wretched tongue of mine."

Beth's face was eager.

"But I could try and change all that, Jodear. If he had his own home and — and children — "

"Bertie doesn't have to work. His

father wallows in money," piped up Lizzie, then added defiantly, with a toss of her head. "If a loved a man like you love Bertie, Beth, I'd fly to Gretna Green with him. Why can't Beth marry the man she loves? I'd rant and rave and what is more, I'd insist that Bertie use his second name. It's so romantic."

"Laurent! Oh no!" shrieked her two sisters.

"I knew that would throw your knickers into a knot," said Lizzie smugly.

"Where on earth did you hear that very vulgar expression?" demanded Joanna.

"From the tweeny."

"Esmeralda?"

Beth's voice was quiet. "Lizzie dear, Mother would be very displeased with you if she could hear you use that awful phrase and another thing, ladies do not fly to Gretna Green, no matter how romantic it might sound."

"Pooh! I would," and blew her

fingers as if the words were so many dandelion clocks.

Freddie with a smile, quietly got up from his chair and said, "What has happened to lessons today, Lizzie?"

"I have the toothache and besides, I don't like lessons. They're boring."

"Well, why don't you go over and see Ruth for a while? She would like a visit from you, I'm sure," giving her a gentle push towards the door.

Lizzie turned around and glared at her sisters. "You are both beasts," and with a flounce slammed the door behind her.

Joanna's snort was unladylike. "How's that for a Sara Siddon's exit? Sometimes I could pin that child's ears back."

Freddie reseated himself astride the chair. A favourite position of his. "Beth, ask Uncle Joseph if he'll allow you to see Bertie, just once more, to say goodbye. Uncle is never unreasonable and anyway, you'll be meeting him at functions. We just can't cut him dead, now can we? He comes from a very good family and, what's more, we've known him all our lives."

Joanna had gone over to Beth and was holding her close, which Beth did not really appreciate.

If only everyone would just leave me alone, she thought, clenching her fingers until the nails bit into her palms. All this was like a harrow over her feelings.

Freddie added gently, "It would be dashed uncomfortable for you if the dibs weren't in tune and bills unpaid. You deserve better than that, Bethie," which did not mend matters at all.

There was another interruption, this time it was Jed, the youngest of Mr. Linnett's sons, a boy of fourteen, who burst into the room, his grey eyes shining, dark hair ruffled and followed by a ragmat of a dog.

"I thought those chestnuts were yours, Freddie. Bang up set of blood and bone!"

"If you run quickly, you'll catch up with Fick before he unharnesses them.

14

Tell him I said you could handle the ribbons, but watch those hands of yours, Jed. My pair have tender mouths," and clapped the boy on the shoulder. "And lock up that hound of yours."

Jed shot out again at a rate of knots, shouting out as he went, "You're a good 'un, Freddie. Thanks."

"Freddie, why did you come over?" asked Joanna. "Did you perhaps bring a message from your mama, or perhaps your papa? Or just to be sociable?"

This was a routine question, for Freddie was a little forgetful on occasions.

"I've just come to make all right and tight. Mother has said she'll chaperon you and Beth to Lady Newton's Ball, on Saturday. Mama has to take Susan, anyway. Jodear, keep me some dances, will you? Waltzes."

"Of course and please thank Aunt Fanny for coming to our rescue. As you know Mother is not fit, these days to take us," then added enthusiastically,

15

"I wouldn't have missed this Ball for the world."

Her shining eyes met his with a complete lack of selfconsciousness. "And you are such a superb dancer, Freddie."

Freddie nodded his head, but his smile held a hint of rue. With a gulped down sigh he took his leave of them wondering when his little friend would realise that he was a grown man now, who was very much in love with her.

The two girls sat silent for a while, after Freddie had left, Joanna breaking that silence. "Were we ever such a problem as Lizzie has become? You know, Bethie, when I get married, I don't want a big family. The children way down the line get neglected."

Beth was aghast. "Jodear! Don't blame Mother. When we were young there were ample servants. More than we have now. Ever since Father's business fell on bad times, Mother has had to take on a lot of duties herself. It is not her fault that we see so little of her."

Joanna nodded and then sighed. She loved this sister of hers and admired her innate poise and dignity that was so appealing, but it was only she who sensed the deep hurt that her parents' refusal of her engagement to Bertie had caused.

In this Joanna was wrong. Mrs. Linnett busy with her numerous household chores was, within weeks, expecting to be delivered of a child, also watched her eldest daughter with loving sympathy, but kept her thoughts to herself. Her husband was right in his decision. Bertie was too unstable and yet a likeable lad, for all that.

* * *

It was the night of the Ball. Joanna pouring water from the ewer into the basin that was decorated with violets, added a small quantity of rose fragrance from a glass bottle.

"Well," she said, putting the stopper back carefully. "When this is finished, no more of this for us. Let's hope that Father makes his fortune, this time, with his new machinery, or else I don't see either of us enjoying any more perfume."

Later, her face in a towel, added. "You'll see Bertie tonight, Bethie and you'll be able to say goodbye. Oh, please don't look like that!"

Beth bit her bottom lip and turned away. "That will change nothing. You have no idea have you, Jodear, what it is like to love someone deeply?"

Joanna shook her head. "When I see how you are suffering, I don't think I want to. Deuced uncomfortable!"

"Joanna!"

But Joanna was unrepentant.

"Jodear, haven't you any deep feelings — feelings for Freddie?"

"Oh, I have. He's the most experienced dancer; I love being in the fields with him, or amongst the animals on the Home Farm; he's a wonderful animal doctor and he's another brother."

Beth had to smile. "And having arguments with him when you disagree with his handling of his workers. You should have been a boy."

Joanna busily tunnelling her way into her evening gown, said with a sigh, "Wish we could have had something new for this occasion."

Her pink dress was very plain, with tiny puffed sleeves and gathered at the waist. She seated herself before the mirror for Beth to do her hair.

"In a topknot, I think," said Beth, "and I'll allow a cascade of ringlets on either side of your face. Your fringe for once, will be in place." But Beth was still unsatisfied. "Your dress is too plain. Wear that necklace your godmother gave you, Jodear. It will make all the difference."

Joanna reached for her trinket box and took out a dainty string of rose quartz flowers entwined with gold leaves.

"What a difference!" said Beth. Her dress was a cream silk that went charmingly with her fair colouring, the top cut low and surrounded by a frill, edged with lace of the same colour, the skirt ending in a deep flounce.

"Bethie, you are beautiful. Here, let me fasten that string of pearls for you. No wonder Bertie wants to marry you, but he must have known that Father would object? I wonder why he even asked?"

Beth was startled. "We love each other, that is why." It was inconceivable that this sister of hers knew absolutely nothing about the tenderest of all emotions.

"Jodear, just you wait," and went across to the cupboard to get her shawl, a lacy spangled affair.

"How would Bertie maintain a household, or hasn't he discussed this with you?"

"He has expectations from his godfather. Now please let us forget about the whole affair," her voice muffled. "My shawl isn't here. Where has it gone? Nothing is going right," she wailed.

Joanna draped the missing shawl across Beth's shoulders. "It was across the chair, you goose."

Beth however, was not pacified. "Oh dear, I'm in such a tizz. What if Bertie is there?"

"Well, you can't disappear down a mousehole, but I thought you did want to see him?"

Beth gathered herself together. "Yes, I do want to speak to him."

The two girls went downstairs to find that Freddie had already arrived looking, as usual, very presentable in black coat and trousers, with a white frilly shirt.

He bowed to them and gave both an arm.

"Two beautiful ladies," then turned and said over his shoulder, "will look after them, Uncle Joseph. Papa and Mama send their regards to you, Sir and to Aunt Eliza."

Freddie helped the girls into the carriage, saw that their dresses would not be too sadly crushed and got in himself.

Mrs. Martin and Susan sat opposite them, Mrs. Martin very matronly in a deep blue gown, while Susan wore a white silk dress with a Bertha collar and blue ribbons around her waist.

Mrs. Martin was always pleased to chaperon these young people to functions as it gave her an opportunity to meet her friends for delightful cozes. She bent forward to take Beth's hand in hers.

"I've been asked by your father, dear, to allow you to dance with Bertie, for as your father pointed out, it would be the height of bad manners for you to refuse him. After all, he is a very old friend of us all." She patted Beth's hand sympathetically. "I know, dear child, that he has offered for you and that your father — Oh, my dear child, don't look like that, but truly it would not be a good match." Mrs. Martin always felt others misfortunes acutely.

"But, Mama, what is Bethie going to do?" asked Susan curiously. "We've known him all our lives. He is of our circle. To see him always is going to be most painful for Beth."

"Nonsense, my dear!" This, from Mrs. Martin, was very firm indeed. "None of us want to see Beth made unhappy. Marrying Bertie would be the way to Weeping Cross."

An uncomfortable silence ensued. Beth sat quite still trying desperately to gulp down her tears, Joanna pressed comfortably against her. Freddie stared out of the window and it came to him, not for the first time, that the evening was going to be far from easy.

"Bertie would be correct if he did not attend this Ball," said Mrs. Martin austerely, which put a stop to Susan's very pertinent questioning.

The carriage stopped at last, much to Beth's relief. The mansion of Lady Newton blazed with light. Freddie handed out his ladies, shepherding them up a flight of wide, shallow steps to the brass studded door, both leaves of which had been thrown open.

The portly butler, dignity personified, advanced in a stately manner to greet them. Bowing he said, "Good evening ladies and gent. Welcome."

They all had a greeting for him, Mrs. Martin enquiring after his wife who had been poorly the last time she had visited this house.

"Master Freddie," he said allowing a smile to appear. "Three beautiful ladies?"

"They all need looking after, Stokes. My evening will be busy. Devilish!"

Joanna's spontaneous, unaffected chuckle caused Stokes to smile again. "Freddie, what a whopper! You love delegating for Uncle Adam."

Mrs. Martin was still a most attractive woman and did not look her age. Her fair hair was unstreaked by grey and her plump figure did not lend itself to wrinkles.

There had been several occasions

where Freddie had had to put his oar in, as he was wont to say, to protect his mama from the too ardent attentions of some aging roué.

Mrs. Martin, with an indignant look at her son sailed into the reception hall, the three young ladies in her train, with Freddie bringing up the rear.

Lady Newton, a tall, imposing figure, robed in majestic purple and gold whose vast bosom held an astonishing amount of jewels, greeted them graciously before they passed through into the enormous ballroom which had been built on to the back of the residence for just such a purpose as this.

Mrs. Martin and the girls stopped and stared. The walls had been lined with pale pink silk and at every corner and under every window baskets of hothouse flowers were tastefully arranged.

"Beautiful, quite beautiful," murmured Mrs. Martin. "Fortunately none of our dresses clash," and made a beeline for a row of vacant chairs, settling herself down comfortably.

"Glad you brought us early, Freddie," she said with a sigh. "There are enough chairs for all of us."

"Oh," breathed Beth to Joanna as she glanced around the room. "What lovely dresses. Look at that redhead over there. Isn't she beautiful and all those glowing emeralds!"

"Our dresses are at least paid for and we have no reason to be envious, Bethie. This is not like you and that redhead does not suit the decor. In fact that hair clashes horribly."

"I'm not being envious, but I would have liked Bertie to have seen me in a beautiful new gown, just once."

"There he is now, over there by the main door. You'll be able to say your adieus. Now hold up your head, Bethie. Here he comes."

"What am I to say or — or do?" she asked with some panic.

"Father has given his permission for you to dance with him and Aunt

26

Fanny is nodding her head. Don't be a goose."

Suddenly all nervous qualms left Beth, leaving her a lovely, glowing girl.

"It will give us an opportunity to talk," and went off happily on his arm.

Freddie led Joanna out for the first dance.

"You look very charming, Jodear, but then everything you wear suits you. It's the enchantment you possess," and grinned at her startled face.

"Are you feeling quite the thing, Freddie?" she asked. "Perhaps something you wish me to do for you? Introduce you to some young lady? Hmm?"

"No, you ass," retorted her lifelong friend. "Really, Jo, you do look very endearing — " He stopped short and sighed. It was no good. Joanna had no inkling of his deep feelings for her. She was as unawakened as the snowdrops under the winter snow.

"My love," he murmured under his

breath. "Snowdrops do spring forth eventually."

"Bertie's here. Did you notice him?"

"Hm! Don't worry. I'll keep an eye on things."

Joanna felt a relieving of her tension. "You are a dear, Freddie. Bertie should not have come."

He agreed. "Pity about his gambling otherwise he's the best of good fellows. Never has a feather to fly with, of course," and swung her deftly into another turn.

What a superb dancer he is, thought Joanna and gave herself up to the magic of one of Herr Strauss' beguiling melodies.

Sometime during the evening Joanna noticed Bertie and Beth slip away out on to the verandah that led to the garden.

"Oh, Gemima!" she gasped and quickly glanced around for Freddie. There he was talking to a friend at the other end of the room. She tapped an impatient foot. Why didn't he look her way? Suddenly he caught her glance and nodded. She sighed with relief and watched as he stationed himself just outside the door through which the young couple had gone.

Aunt Fanny had also noticed and appeared to be satisfied which left Joanna free to accept her next partner, a lanky shy son of their hostess.

"Why, Kenneth, your dancing has really improved. What a nice surprise," and smiled kindly up at him.

"Thank you, Miss Joanna," blushing to the roots of his hair, his pale eyebrows standing out in sharp relief. "M'sister has taken me in hand. Sorry to hear about your father's troubles. Bad business, workers smashing machinery. Not on, really, now is it?"

"Don't let's talk," she replied. "This music is too beautiful for that."

"Suits me. Not one for much chin-wagging," and blushed again wondering if he had committed a social solecism.

★ ★ ★

Bertie placed a protecting arm about Beth's shoulders as they made their way into the garden and said, "A shocking squeeze this. Lady Newton must be in high fettle," and led Beth to a seat. "You are so sweet and fresh, Bethie," taking her into his arms and holding her close. "I'm at rest when I'm with you. Oh, Bethie!" With a groan he released her. "Sorry, I've no more right to do that."

Her hand curled in his, Beth said eagerly, "You could change, dearest. I know you could and I — I wouldn't mind so much if you gambled a little every now and again."

"Oh, Beth, I'm not worthy of you, my little love. I'll love you all my life, you know that don't you, but gambling is in my blood. My grandfather was the same, he practically ruined the family."

The moon silvered his fair head and Beth felt a catch in her throat. How very dear he was.

"Bertie, if you truly loved me, you

30

could make an effort, surely?"

"Too late. Your father is correct. I'm not the husband for you. What if I left you night after night. No!" He sighed. "I've tried to stop the habit. Forget me, Bethie," and held his head in his hands.

"I don't think I could ever do that, dearest."

"The music has stopped. We must go in."

Was there relief in his words, wondered Beth sadly as he led her back to Mrs. Martin.

Only Joanna had noticed that Freddie had come in at the door after them.

One glance at Beth's face made Mrs. Martin hold out her hand and take Beth's unresisting fingers warmly into her own which made Beth give thanks for this dear adopted aunt. No words were necessary but she was very conscious of the sympathy pouring over her hurt like a benediction and was grateful too, that no trite platitudes were offered.

The music stopped again and Joanna came off the floor to take Beth up the wide branched staircase that rose to the gallery above and hence to the Powder Room.

By the time Beth had washed her face and tidied her hair she had regained much of her composure to allow Joanna to say gently, "I don't think Father would have liked you to go out into the garden with Bertie."

"How could anyone have had a rational talk in all that noise? Oh Jodear, I asked him if he couldn't try and give up gambling for — for me." She shook her head.

As a sob broke from her Joanna gathered her close. "Oh, Bethie I'm sorry!"

"He — he didn't even want to try. I don't think he truly loves me, but that doesn't change my love."

Joanna slipped a comforting hand into Beth's. "Come, wash your face again. We must go down. Can't let the tongues wag."

The rest of the evening was a nightmare for Beth as she danced and smiled as if nothing had happened. She was quick to notice, though, that Bertie had left the Ball soon after their talk and this had given back some of her confidence.

It was a silent journey back to Jade Place, Mrs. Martin, Freddie and Joanna silently applauding the white faced girl, slumped in the corner of the carriage, her adieu smile a travesty of truth.

★ ★ ★

April had given way to May and a succession of spring days had brought colour to the wild flowers and hedges of the countryside. Beth and Joanna escaped out of the house as often as their household duties allowed, both keenly aware of the lush green of trees and fields; the blossom of cherry and pear, scattering their petals in wild disorder.

Joanna would dare Beth and they

would catch up their hampering skirts and run to the top of the hill as if seven devils were at their backs, arriving back home again hot and dishevelled but gloriously alive.

One Monday morning as Joseph Linnett was looking through his mail with his secretary, one Michael Turner, a bright, pleasant faced young man, with a pleasing appearance, there came a knock on the door and Squire Martin came in.

"Good morning, Joseph," he boomed, "and to you, young Turner," who returned his smile.

"Come in, come in, Adam," replied Mr. Linnett, shaking his old friend by the hand. "Sit down, please, but excuse us for a second," handing Mr. Turner a sheaf of papers. "Michael, take these orders through and see that all the customers' requirements are strictly adhered to. These answer. I'll leave the rest to you. There's a good chap," settling himself in his chair.

"Nice lad, Turner. Don't know what

I'd do without him. Good upbringing always counts. Now friend, is this a social call or what?"

"Joseph, I'm asking you with no bark on it, how is your business doing?"

If there was a slight stiffening in Mr. Linnett's body, the Squire was unaware of it.

"'The day your horse dies and your money's lost,'" quoted Joseph quietly.

"Another of your Chinese proverbs, I presume? Not as bad as that, surely, dear friend?"

"No, no. Matters have settled down again after that last ruction."

"You mean after the workers had smashed all your new machinery?"

Mr. Linnett nodded and sighed. "Poor souls. I can see their point of view, Adam. They all feel their jobs are at risk and who can blame them?"

"Yes, yes, but this Industrial Revolution is here to stay. It's been going on for some time now, anyway. Nothing is ever static in this life. I, as you know, installed new threshing machines and have had no problems."

"Then why me?" asked Joseph throwing out his arms.

"Well, I was very careful to assure my workers that their wages would remain the same and, of course, all my workers have been with me for years as their fathers before them. Plus the fact that we give them good housing, which you are unable to supply. That's the difference, no doubt."

Mr. Linnett owned a fabric printing manufactory in the business sector of London, employing a fair number of workers. He was a quiet, bookish man, tall whitehaired, with blue eyes and yet he was a most progressive man, buying the latest machinery — new fangled — his wife called them — from the United States. It was his quiet tenacity that had made his business a lucrative one that is, until he bought the new machinery.

His dealings with his workers were always fair and on Sunday afternoons held classes for his workers' children, where they were not only taught from the Bible, but also to read and write. Both Beth and Joanna were willing helpers. This gave the children a chance in life and to get them off the streets.

Some said that Mr. Linnett was teaching them to be revolutionaries, others said that they would get ideas above their station, but the Sunday afternoons flourished.

Joseph's expression was sheepish. "Perhaps you'll think me a fool, Adam, but I've ordered more machinery from the States. In fact, they are at the wharf now."

"That's brave of you, but was that wise?" asked the surprised Squire, his eyebrows working furiously.

"I want to be part of this mechanised age, Adam. It's different, it's exciting. That is why I'm willing to try again, but I must admit that it is the older workers that don't take kindly to change. I've given my word again that no worker will be dismissed, that the machinery will make their lives easier, if they will only give it a chance. I have great hope that this time no trouble will occur. They're also afraid that I won't take on any men when others leave."

"That's laudable, thinking of their fellow creatures. So be it, Joseph." An uneasy silence fell only broken by the arrival of the teatray brought in by Michael.

As the two old friends drank their tea, Joseph enquired after the Squire's eldest son, Paul.

"Have you heard from him? Still Army mad?"

The Squire accepted the change of subject.

He was a bluff hearty man, beetling eyebrows overhung keen dark eyes that missed nothing and as far as the Linnett family were concerned, did not mind his own business. In fact, he treated all the Linnett children as if they were his own, who often complained that the Squire was downright overpowering.

For a moment sadness crossed his features as he thought of his son.

"No news is good news, so the Sages say, but then when did ever Paul write? He's my heir, as you well know, Joseph, but can you imagine him running the Home Farm as Freddie has done for years?"

Mr. Linnett shook his head. "One day Paul will come home and settle down," he soothed, watching the Squire fiddling with those bushy eyebrows and thought, with amusement, that Fanny had not had a go at that lush wilderness for some time. She must be very busy or just not noticed.

"I'm concerned about Freddie, Joseph. What's his future?"

"Buy him a farm, Adam."

The Squire threw out his hand. An over simplification. "He'd need a wife." His manner softened. "I want Joanna for a daughter-in-law."

"I also wish for a match there as much as you do. Freddie would be welcomed into my family like a shot, but — have you ever watched those two together? My Jodear has no inkling of

39

Freddie's love for her. She is totally unaware of feelings woman has for man."

"Freddie is just another brother. I know. I know," sighed the Squire morosely.

Two weeks later the new machinery was duly installed. Mr. Linnett came home for luncheon hopeful that this time his workers would accept the situation and boosted up his spirits by thinking of other businesses, that after initial teething problems, had settled down nicely. This was progress. During the luncheon though, he did admit that the papers still received angry letters from their readers.

Mrs. Linnett mentioned a few. "'The unwashed masses now would mingle with the upper classes.' How they came to that conclusion, I don't know. 'Armageddon just around the corner.' The people are angry, Joseph."

"Yes, my love, I know, but quietly changes are being made for the betterment of the people."

"But," insisted his wife whose sympathies lay with their work staff, "there have been a lot of riots which show their fear. Poor things!" She sighed. "Fear, is a motifying force in all of us, Joseph, and does not, sometimes listen to reason. My dear, I do hope you'll have no more troubles." In a more cheerful voice she turned to her family and excused them from the table.

That afternoon, latish, Joanna was sitting on the windowseat watching the old lamplighter make his way down their street. It was a raw misty afternoon and the gas lamps put out an eerie light.

Beth had just lit the table lamp and said with a worried frown, "Papa was so filled with hope at luncheon. Wonder what the situation is like at the manufactory?"

"Perhaps this time, he'll be able to keep his new machinery intact. Father certainly perseveres." Joanna was still watching the old man and she suddenly chuckled. "Remember how Nanny used to terrify us when we were small, threatening to give us away to the old lamplighter if we didn't behave ourselves? Now I welcome that muffled figure lighting up our road. I'm worried now though, Bethie."

Mrs. Linnett entered the schoolroom. Her condition showed that she hadn't much more time to go.

Beth got up hurriedly, slipped an arm around her mother's thickened waist and guided her to a chair.

"Don't you think you should be on your bed, Mama dear?" she asked gently.

"Bless you, no, my dearest. Being on one's feet helps, so they say." She suddenly looked worn out.

"Sit down, Mother," said Beth, pulling out the pins that held the heavy bun of sable hair, which Jed had inherited, and brushed it with soothing strokes.

Mrs. Linnett's voice was barely audible. "That's enough thank you."

"Ah, here's the teatray," said Joanna thankfully. Her mother looked very unwell. She helped the little maid to set the small table, spreading out the lace edged cloth and arranging the large plate of sandwiches with its crocheted doyley.

The tweeny bobbed a curtsy before scuttling from the room.

"Maids seem to get younger by the year," observed Mrs. Linnett, thankfully accepting the cup of tea from Joanna.

"And when you have finished that, Mama, we'll help you to your room and call Nanny."

"Yes, Jodear. I — I think I'll go now."

Both girls had just returned to their tea when the tweeny came in again, twisting her hands in a not too clean apron.

"Please, Miss Jodear, Nurse wants you immediate," and rushed from the room, with Joanna at her heels.

As Joanna ran along the passage,

down the staircase and through the hall, she noticed that the Chippendale table, with its clustered legs, had disappeared.

With a sigh she sped on towards the kitchens in the wake of Esmeralda. The whole family had all learnt not to comment on missing items of furniture. It had all started when her father's business had deteriorated when his new machinery had been smashed. Both she and Beth had guessed then that money was becoming scarce.

In the kitchen Mr. and Mrs. Swales and Nanny were gathering food into hampers. Joanna stopped, looking completely bewildered. "I — I thought it was Mother. Nanny?"

"No, she'll do for the time being. Jodear, your father's in trouble. It's those dratted workers again."

She paused to come across to Joanna, putting her hands on to her shoulders. "John Coachman has just been in. Your mother isn't fit to hear all this. I'll not tell her. If I see the signs correctly, she'll be in labour tonight. Oh, Jodear, please go to your father and see what is happening. I — I thought if you could get all the children off the floors, it would help. I don't like sending you, it's not proper and that's a fact, but — "

"Of course I'll go, Nanny," she soothed and began to help with the packing, "but why the food? And what on earth will I be able to do?"

"Children can be destructive, could inflame men already hot headed," she replied. "Now, my dearie, get those children into that big storeroom. They could make the situation worse."

"There's not a lot of food in these two small hampers," put in Mrs. Swales, gloomily, "and none of us will get our supper this night."

"The children will be grateful for whatever you have put in those baskets, but what on earth can I really do?" asked Joanna again.

"Make those children sit down and feed them. That should help. Here, child," and Nanny threw a long, warm cape over Joanna's shoulders. "May the Lord protect you and the Master. Now keep that hood down over your face."

"So no one will recognise me?" she asked mischievously.

"Get on with you, Jodear."

"What will people say if they see you out by yourself?" quavered old Mr. Swales. "And in that area, too."

"Once you have those children in that storeroom, don't forget to shut the door." This from Mrs. Swales who was also looking extremely worried.

Joanna nodded. "I'll barricade us all in. Please don't worry about me."

"Not worry about you, Miss Jodear?" cried Mrs. Swales, with a failing voice. "Oh dear! I'm going to have palpitations."

"No you won't," ordered her husband, usually the meekest of men.

Mrs. Swales' mouth dropped ludicrously and her "No, dearie," was the mildest she had uttered for many a year and began to help Nanny to fasten the hampers.

"John Coachman should be here any minute now. Why did Mr. Douglas have to be away just now," worried Nanny.

"He had to go. You know he's gone up North to get orders for the business."

Nanny grunted. "John Coachman is reliable. Oh dear! Have I been right in sending you off like this?"

"Any sweets, Nanny? Let's have them too," suggested Joanna.

At that moment John came in and the hampers were loaded into the carriage. Joanna was on her way.

Once that was done, Nanny, the Swales and the tweeny sat down to a welcome cup of tea, all fearful of what the ensuing hours would bring.

Putting her cup down, Nanny got up from her chair slower than usual. She felt unutterably tired.

"Now I must go and see the Mistress. It's bed for her. I've been turned every which way this evening."

Maggie Brown, a tall woman, with

fine grey hair that continually slithered out from a mass of hairpins, had been with the family for more years than she cared to admit, but, for her, they had been busy, happy years and she had no complaints. All the children loved her and the girls would borrow her hairpins, that made the basis for making little dolls, which they made with surprising ease and originality.

★ ★ ★

As Joanna had climbed into the carriage she said, "Please, John, drop me a little way from the manufactory. You just might have trouble with the workers and you could be hurt. I — I wouldn't have that happen for the world. It wouldn't help me or father."

"No argufication, Miss Jodear. I'm taking you to the backdoor and that's that, but how Maggie thinks a slip of a girl like you can help — "

"But I'm sure I can."

"How, Missie?"

48

"This is Nanny's idea. Get all the children off the floors. I'll not even show my face in there. I'll ask Mary to shepherd all the young ones into that large storeroom, where all the dyes and cloth are stored and then I'll feed them," she ended up triumphantly. "It'll work. It's got to."

The old man had grunted as he climbed up on to his seat, gathering the reins into his calloused hands.

They drove through unsavoury suburbs that were overcrowded in the extreme, with unwashed, ragged humanity milling around the streets. Joanna shuddered at their plight.

The mist of the late afternoon had dispersed and the moon rising, bathed the dark, dismal streets with liquid silver, softening austere outlines of dilapidated buildings, gentling the squalor and lending them a ghostly beauty that was never seen in the light of day.

As Joanna was driven along, her thoughts turned to the children who worked for her father. She knew them, each and every one, their dreams and fears; a hard father or a sick mother who depended on the pittance they took home. Her father paid higher wages than most businesses, but still their situation was sad.

In her concern, Joanna forgot that her own family went without some of the basics of life. She was jolted out of her reverie, as the carriage stopped and John opened the door for her. They unloaded the baskets and took them into the storeroom.

Joanna accompanied John to the door.

"I'll have to leave you now, Miss Jodear. Must take the carriage to the Inn. I'll be right back. Can't leave the horses standing here. Like as not they would be stolen."

As he turned to mount, Joanna laid a hand on his arm. "Please John, ask Mary to come to the storeroom. Nanny said I hadn't to be seen by the men. I had almost forgot."

Mary soon arrived, an undersized child, whose whole face radiated a smile of welcome when she saw Joanna, who hugged her and told her what was required of her.

"Bring all the children to this room. Tell them I've brought a picnic supper. That should draw them."

"Right, Miss Jo. They're getting some'ut under the men's feet." Mary might be undersized but was very much alert to the whole situation.

By twos and threes the children arrived, curious to see what this was all about, but when they saw the baskets, were willing enough to sit down and listen to Joanna.

"First of all, we're going to march, march for our supper, around and around this room. When we are tired we're all going to have something to eat. Up you get and start marching and singing at the top of your voices. Now, please."

"Right, Miss," they all chorused and with Joanna in the lead and Mary bringing up the rear, their shrill little voices reached the roof.

> "'Onward Christian soldiers
> Marching as to war,
> Looking unto Jesus
> Who has gone before.'"

"And take those sullen looks off your faces," yelled Joanna. "Smile and move. Quicker, quicker!" Round and round they all went.

> "'Forth to the mighty conflict
> In this His glorious day.'"

Not an entirely felicitous theme, mused Joanna and suppressed a giggle. "Louder. Louder. March, children," but the children were tiring. "Just once more around the room and you'll have your supper."

The children collapsed on the floor. The baskets were opened and eager, skinny hands held out for the food. A blissful silence reigned, allowing

Joanna's thoughts to turn to her father.

Suddenly she scrambled to her feet, as a tall masked figure brought in a little girl, holding her by the hand and approached her. For the life of her she could not move.

Standing there in the flickering light of the lamps, they faced each other for a moment in silence, the tall man clothed wholly in black, hat drawn well down over his face and the slender girl with honeybrown hair, her fresh young face upturned to his where fear widened her deep blue eyes.

Eyes glittered through the mask and Joanna's fear subsided. Those eyes were laughing.

The stranger said gruffly, "Well done, little one. Keep them on the move after that meal, until they drop." Like the unerring swoop of a kingfisher on the river, his mouth came down on hers. A quick, hard kiss and he was gone.

Joanna stared at the open doorway, her heart beating uncomfortably fast and felt she'd been swept up by a strong force that, somehow, seemed to have taken over her liberty.

"Rubbish!" she snorted out aloud as she came to her senses. None of the children had taken the least bit of notice of the stranger and were steadily demolishing the contents of the baskets. Had it been a dream? It was most peculiar. Was the stranger known to them? And that little girl he had brought in? She had shown no fear.

Curiosity got the better of her and she called Mary over to her. "Who was that man who came in just now? Do you know?"

Mary shrugged her thin shoulders. "Don't rightly know, Miss," her mouth full of bread, her fingers clutching a sweet. "Just the Stranger, Miss. Please don't ask me anymore," and joined the other children, leaving Joanna more and more intrigued.

Her thoughts turned to her father. The noise and shouting had died down.

* * *

Much, much later, when all the children
and the workers had left, Mr. Linnett,
Michael Turner and John, came into
the storeroom to find Joanna huddled
on a bale of cloth, nearly asleep. She
managed to scramble to her feet as
the men came in and rushed into her
father's arms.

"Oh, I've been so frightened," her
tired body trembling.

"Jodear, you did a sterling job
tonight, keeping all those children out
of the way. Well done, my dear."

"It was Nanny's idea."

"Then blessings to Nanny, a woman
in a thousand. Now come home,
everyone. Turner, join us if you will.
A hot cup of chocolate would be most
beneficial. John, please take us home.
My grateful thanks to you all."

Michael declined the offer, saying
that his parents would be worrying
about him and Mr. Linnett once again
expressed his thanks.

★ ★ ★

When they reached home, only Nanny was in the kitchen and was able to give them a report on Mrs. Linnett, after she had heard their news.

"I'm just taking a cup of tea up to her. Perhaps, Sir, you'd like to join her. You all look so weary."

Mr. Linnett nodded. "Chocolate for us, Nanny please, if it is not too much bother. John will have some too."

"His wife will see to that. She'll be glad to see him home. We've been that worried. Doctor has been. I thought it wise. He's just left. Another couple of hours, he said."

Nanny turned to Joanna.

"Thank you, child. I was at my wits end to know what to do for the best. Now it's bed for you."

"Your idea worked beautifully. That food was soon gone, but I had an idea of my own. I made them march until they dropped with tiredness." A

56

little smile of remembrance touched her tired face.

Turning to her father she said, "May I speak to you before you go up to mother?" Her father nodded and she went on. "A masked man brought a child into the storeroom this evening. Did he have anything to do with the workers being more amenable to the situation? Who is he, Papa?"

"Do you see him as a romantic figure, Jodear?" His quirky smile was very much in evidence. "And you such a tomboy?"

"Nothing of the sort, Father, please stop teasing."

Mr. Linnett wondered, interestedly, whether his daughter's repudiation had come out a little too quickly to be natural.

"I'm curious, that's all. Not one of those children showed the slightest concern and he was masked. Mary refused to discuss him. Intriguing!"

"Do you see him in the role of a modern Robin Hood?"

"You're hedging, Father."

"Jodear, that stranger, whoever he may be, was most helpful in calming down the men. I'm very much obliged to him. More than you'll ever know," he sighed and went on. "I don't know who he is, but I do know that he has helped several of the families. Respect his anonymity, Jodear and it's time you were in bed, anyway, my dear."

"Oh Father, how thoughtless of me. You look so weary. I shouldn't be keeping you up."

"I must go and see your mother, bless her. It's been quite a day for all of us. I'll sit with her until Nanny kicks me out."

Mr. Linnett went upstairs and along to the bedroom, took his wife's hand in his. "My poor love. Soon will be all over," he comforted and kissed her flushed cheek.

Joanna made her way wearily up to her room and went to the window to gaze out on to a sleeping world, long shadows cast by a pale moon.

She could not get that tall slim stranger out of her mind. Who was he and why were the children keeping quiet about him? What a curious encounter? Romantic? But she was not a romantic and crawled into bed, but the stranger remained at the back of her eyelids. Remembered again her moments of panic, the fear subsiding and his words. "Well done, little one," laughter in his eyes as he said it.

Joanna was suddenly aware of feelings she had never experienced before and shied away from them, but as she fell asleep, her last memories were of the stranger, his black cloak swirling around him as he left the storeroom; and that kiss?

★ ★ ★

Later that night the workers went back and utterly destroyed the new machinery and early the next morning, Mrs. Linnett was delivered of a child. The little girl was named Sarah.

2

SEVERAL mornings later, Joseph was sitting on the bed. Eliza had recovered well, he thought, searching that dear familiar face and took a deep breath. He was yet to break the news of this latest catastrophe that had befallen them and was finding it difficult to find the appropriate words. His voice was raw and abrupt when they eventually came out.

"All gone! All gone," and quietly told her what had happened.

Eliza was aghast. "Oh, Joseph, my dear!" holding out her hand to him. "What dreadful news! I'm so sorry," clutching the baby more closely to her breast.

"This — this shock won't dry up your milk, will it, my love?" his eyes anxious.

"No no. It won't. Isn't she a little

dear?" No words of censor, no anger, just a quiet acceptance. 'Man with the head and woman with the heart, man commands and woman to obey. All else confusion' fleetingly came to her mind.

Joseph knew that his wife was very aware of their parlous monetary position, felt a stab of guilt. It was his blame, his overriding ambition to move forward into the future on the heels of this revolution that had brought them to this predicament.

Eliza went on. "We're very blessed with our children, Joseph. Let's not forget that."

"A quiverful, yes, my dear, yes, but what am I going to do now?" His head sank into his hands, a worried frown between his deep blue eyes which had been inherited by Joanna and Douglas.

"I feel that I've let down my entire family badly, not to mention my workers," then hastened to add, "this urge within me to emulate what

61

others are trying to do, this — this is what has brought about our downfall. My overwhelmingly conceit that I could succeed where others have failed."

Eliza looked startled.

"You'll go on as before, Joseph, surely? With your old machinery?" laying a comforting hand on his shoulder. "You're speaking as if you're totally finished. That's not so."

"But all around me are businesses that are mechanizing. A lot have had troubles, I know and even some have gone under but a few have succeeded. Adam is one them, as we well know, Eliza."

"'There is nothing either good or bad but thinking makes it so'" she quoted softly, then bit her lip hard to stop the hasty words that could have been said.

"Thinking won't take our troubles away, my love," he said ruefully. "I have no more capital to buy more machinery and this forward movement must come about sooner than later. I wanted, more than anything, to be part of that progress."

"Well, dear," Eliza said bracingly. "You still have all your old machinery. In the past we've made a comfortable living from them."

It was patently an obvious relief to Joseph when suddenly, after a sharp knock, the bedroom door was thrown open and Joanna came in followed by Beth with a teatray, which she placed on the bedside table.

"Tea, Father and Mother?" she asked, starting to pour out while Joanna held out her arms, reached down for the baby and went over to the windowseat.

"Isn't she beautiful?" gathering the little bundle close to her then uncurling a tiny fist.

"Thank you, dear." Mrs. Linnett took the cup Beth held out to her and passed it to Joseph, then accepted hers. Beth sat on the bed close to her father who smiled at her, passing an arm around her shoulders.

"Mother, wasn't Jodear absolutely wonderful the way she organised those children and kept them off the floors?"

"It turned out to be a wasted effort," retorted Joanna sharply. "It did not stop the mayhem afterwards."

Mrs. Linnett suddenly sat up in bed. "Joseph, do you mean to say that Joanna was at the manufactory that night? How could you have allowed it! In that awful area — at night. What will people say?"

The words spilled out. It was a relief to be able to vent her anger and disapproval that she had been bottling up since Joseph had told her the news of their latest misfortune.

Joseph clasped her hand. "Please don't be so angry. Think of the little one. It was not my idea. Jodear, thank you. It was most helpful not having those children under our feet and I'm exceedingly grateful for what you did," with a conspiratorial smile in her direction.

Joanna had hoped he would not

mention the stranger. She hadn't even told Beth about him.

"Mother, it was Nanny and Mrs. Swales who thought up the idea. They were absolutely splendid and so was John Coachman, but he did mutter rather a lot and wasn't in favour of the idea at all. It was he who called Mary and she brought the children to that storeroom at the back where we had a picnic, but only after I had made the children march until they were practically dropping."

Beth shuddered, but said bravely, "I would have gone with you, Jodear."

"Yes, I know you would have, but we didn't want the news to reach Mother. If we were both missing Lizzie would have given the game away."

Mrs. Linnett had recovered her poise and said, "Jodear, you should have been a boy."

"No," said Beth forcefully. "Jodear is the best of my sisters. I can't spare her. She's the strong one against my weakness, always sure of herself, while

I — I dither along somehow, anyhow," thinking of Bertie.

"Oh, my dear," murmured Mrs. Linnett patting Beth's hand. "What would we do without our Beth? You know we all love you dearly. You'll one day be a lovely caring wife and mother."

Mr. Linnett drew her close to him. His small mouse, he thought lovingly. Since the initial, financial crash she had made most of the clothes for herself and the rest of the family. His arm tightened around her to find that she had lost weight and some of her bloom. His heart ached for her.

"Your mother speaks the truth, Bethie. You have a tender, loving heart, my dear."

"I won't ever get married now." Her words were barely audible.

"Beth, please try and understand, dear," pleaded her mother. "We only want the best for you. Bertie is a dear lad, one we've known all his life, but at present, he hasn't an ounce of responsibility. Perhaps in the years to come, he'll gain that. I sincerely hope so, for his own sake and that of his family."

Beth's mouth hardened uncharacteristically. "I'll wait for that day then," and turned her face into her father's shoulder and wept.

★ ★ ★

Mr. Linnett's business was soon back on its old footing. The broken machinery had been cleared away, with never another word spoken about the affair, by workers or by management, but Mr. Linnett was both edgy and unsettled.

On this particular morning he'd just had a meeting with a prospective buyer and it was with some apprehension when he looked up to see Squire Martin walk in at the door, just as Michael, his secretary, brought in the teatray. He said abruptly, "I think I might have a buyer for the business."

"What? but — but — " stuttered

Adam, tottering to a chair. "What will you do then, Joseph?"

He met his old friend's bewildered gaze with a steady look. "Last night Eliza and I had a long talk and we've decided the best plan for us is to emigrate to Australia. You remember her two brothers are out there. Went years ago and write glowing letters about the country." The words had come out too quickly and he waited for the reaction.

"Are you mad?" roared Adam. The shock was almost too much for him. His face became livid and his hands shook.

Mr. Linnett quickly poured out a strong cup of tea and handed it to him. The Squire gulped it down, Mr. Linnett grasping his shoulder with sympathy.

"A horrible shock, Adam. I'm sorry. I haven't really taken in the full implications of it myself."

"What has Eliza to say about this hairbrained scheme of yours?"

"She'll fall in with whatever I decide, bless her."

"Aye 'Wherever you go, I'll go,' but Joseph — "

"I must admit she has her reservations — "

"And what were they, I may ask?"

"Well," replied Joseph, not quite meeting his old friend's eyes. "According to her brothers the standards over there have dropped somewhat, but still they say it's a great country."

"Such as?"

"Well, people, some people pick their chops and chicken bones at the table and even at Government House, apparently, there are some who are not very particular which cutlery they use. Little things like that, but perhaps those brothers of Eliza's could be trying to shock her. I wouldn't put it past them."

The Squire snorted. "Eliza will have none of that, I'll be bound."

Joseph went on eagerly. "But there is a wide open field for all types of business ventures and wonderful stories of danger and daring. The racing is good and is conducted like a huge teaparty."

"You don't go in for racing, neither does Eliza."

"But we will be populating one of the outposts of the Empire," replied Joseph with a twinkle.

Adam laughed halfheartedly. "We're all going to miss you and the family damnably." He was surprised at the sense of annoyance that filled him, that the friendship of many years and well ordered lives were to be torn asunder. He kept his feelings under strict control, which was not easy with his peppery temper.

Mr. Linnett agreed wholeheartedly. "We're also going to miss the Martin family, dear friend and when the time comes, I'll hate leaving England and all that I hold dear."

The Squire suddenly sat up.

"Do you realize, Joseph, that my family will be halved?" he said with strong indignation.

Mr. Linnett smiled faintly. "I'm well aware, Adam, that on occasions you really haven't known who were your children and who were mine."

"Well, dash it all, Joseph, they've all tumbled in and out of our respective houses ever since they were born. They've shared the same tutors, girls and boys. It was your idea that our sons would learn quicker with competition from our daughters. I love them all dearly," he added his voice rough.

"And corrected and spanked them equally when necessary. Thank you, Adam."

The two aging gentlemen drank their second cups of tea, Adam saying regretfully, "Can't expect Fanny to supply any more. I spoke to her on this matter when Eliza was expecting this last time and was very smartly told 'No'. I like a little one in the cradle, Joseph," he added plaintively.

Mr. Linnett chuckled, pleased that

the conversation had taken a lighter tone. "Remember the time you came rushing across to Jade Place demanding to see your daughter as you had just found out that she had danced three times with some whippersnapper, in a scarlet coat, at some dance or other?"

The Squire smiled. "Only to find that it was your daughter. Anyway the siblings know who's who, thank goodness. Can't have you taking one of mine across to Australia with you. There was a pause then the Squire went on. "Fanny and I would like you all to come across tomorrow for afternoon tea. It will give everyone an opportunity to discuss this dreadful move of yours."

The invitation was gladly accepted. "Thank you, Adam, it will give the children time to discuss it. Wonder what their reactions will be?"

"Mine will be frankly envious. Yours? The promise of a sea journey to the other side of the world, who could cavil at that? It's Eliza and Nanny who will have qualms. You will be taking Nanny?"

Mr. Linnett nodded. "Couldn't get on without her."

As the Squire left he gave Joseph a hard stare and said, "You have an incurable optimistic disposition, my friend, which, perhaps, leads you astray. Be careful, won't you?"

"You mean it was unwise of me to invest in all that new machinery?"

"Well, you were doing very nicely before you launched into this new venture. You just did not have enough to offer your workers. A little loose screwish?"

Mr. Linnett agreed a little sheepishly and then added, "Perhaps over in Australia people will be more amenable to new inventions. I sincerely hope so."

★ ★ ★

As the Squire drove home his thoughts turned to Joanna. After Joseph, he

73

would miss her the most. Jodear, that piece of quicksilver, that sunbeam. Pictures formed in his mind which took him back down and across the years. Jodear, her honeybrown hair always unruly, scampering about the place, her childish voice shouting, "Uncle Adam! Come see! Come see!" and together they would inspect a bird's nest, or a family of voles that lived on his section of a small stream and wondered, for the hundredth time, whether Jodear and Freddie, would ever make a match of it. How happy Fannie and he would be if this came about. They could never find a sweeter daughter-in-law or Freddie a bride.

Unfortunately he had never seen a trace of consciousness in her deep blue eyes, that she viewed his son other than a dear friend. And now Joseph was emigrating to the other side of the world. What a pity!

Nanny was another who did not view the move kindly and dire forebodings were foretold.

"Traipsing off like that? And what about the children and Sarah so young?" She wagged a finger at Mr. Linnett. "And all those heathen over there?"

"But, Nanny, a lot of British have settled there," he replied and smiled when she retorted sharply. "Well, I'll always have my hatpins with me and umbrella. I'll not hesitate to use them either."

★ ★ ★

The whole family walked over to the Martins' house the following afternoon. It was a pleasant walk, which had been undertaken many times over the years by children and adults alike. Past a stand of trees, past a pasture where cows tranquilly grazed or drowsed in the afternoon sunshine. The whole property spoke of prosperity.

"Adam is very fortunate in having Freddie," observed Mr. Linnett to his wife as they strolled arm in arm, enjoying the mild exercise.

"What will be his future, Joseph? I often worry about him. Paul will have no idea how to manage this estate when it comes into his hands and no interest either. Freddie has worked so hard all these years."

"I have a surprise for you, my sweet. Adam has bought our house for Freddie. Saw Adam about it this morning, but please don't mention it. Adam will tell Fanny at an appropriate moment later. He hopes it will help her to accept this move of ours."

Mrs. Linnett stopped, laying her head on his shoulder, hugging his arm against her more tightly. "Oh, Joseph, what a splendid idea. I've been hating the idea of strangers taking over our dear Jade Place." She lifted her head and showed him a glowing face then bent forward to kiss his cheek, before continuing their stroll in quiet contentment. "Oh, there are Fanny and Adam come out to meet us."

The disquiet in her voice made her

husband say with a chuckle, "I'm sure they didn't see us, but why shouldn't they see you kiss me, anyway?"

The Squire and Mrs. Martin had also been drawn out of doors by the lovely afternoon and had also been discussing Freddie.

What a dear son he was, thought Fanny with gratitude of the boy of the past and the man he had become. Why couldn't Jodear see him as her loving heart saw him. What a wonderful pair they would make.

★ ★ ★

The Martins' residence was Georgian, compact with an air of quiet dignity, the gardens well laid out and maintained, with lawns and shrubs, where the children played endless games and harassed the old gardener. A splendid oak tree avenue served for the main entrance to this fine property.

The two families went into the huge drawingroom and when everyone was settled Mr. Linnett broke the news to them. It was greeted with horrified gasps of unbelief after a moment of unnerving silence.

Before anyone could find a word to say, the Squire held up a hand and suggested, "I think all you children should go out into the garden and discuss this — this unexpected and — words fail me. Off you go."

Mrs. Martin was still speechless. She appeared to have shrunk in her chair. Adam had not broken the news to her.

It was Mrs. Linnett who first broke the silence. "Douglas and Eva send their regrets. I was hoping they could have been here too. This has hit Douglas hard."

"Fortunately the new owners of the business are willing to keep Douglas on as he knows all the customers so well," said Mr. Linnett.

"We'll miss them and you all so much," murmured Mrs. Linnett, with a quiver in her voice.

"I'd like to suggest that you two ladies go off too, to discuss this — this — " The Squire could not go on, still groping for an adequate word to describe his feelings which would be suitable for the ears of the ladies.

Mrs. Martin took her friend up to her boudoir where she threw herself on to the day couch and burst into tears.

"But — but why are you going, Eliza?"

"Joseph seems to think that we'll do better in Australia. You know my brothers are out there and — and we are bankrupt."

She took the still weeping Fanny into her arms. "Hush dear, you'll make yourself ill."

"Oh, Eliza, what am I going to do without you?"

"And I you, dear friend," she replied sadly, biting her under lip to stop it trembling.

"I've relied on you ever since we were at school together. I'll never forget how you took a scared thirteen year old and fought her battles for her. I hated school before you arrived at Miss Harford's School for Young Ladies. Oh!" Another wail broke from Fanny.

Eliza said quietly, but firmly, "Fanny sit up, dear. Come, let me mop you up. There, is that better?" Fanny nodded. "Now we'll talk this through like two rational beings. I need it as much as you do. You're no longer a lonely, frightened little girl, but a woman with a dear, loving husband. He's a tower of strength, Fanny, and what about your children?"

These two ladies were as different as chalk from cheese, in temperament and also in looks. Fanny fair, plump and blue eyed, whilst Eliza was of darker colouring with a much more forthright approach to life.

"I know, I know I'm blessed," murmured Fanny.

"I hate the idea as much as you do and have had to conceal my true feelings, as I certainly don't want this upheaval either, but I have bowed to Joseph's decision." Eliza sighed. "I had visions of my grandchildren running in and out of Jade Place."

"And mine, too," agreed Fanny with quivering lips and another burst of tears, which she tried to wipe away with a dainty wisp of cotton and lace. "And another matter, Eliza," with a hiccup, "Adam is very worried about Paul. He has refused to come home. He should be here learning to run the Home Farm, but we had a letter at the beginning of the week. All he's interested in are his horses, his *remuda* he calls them. Adam and I are also fearful that when he comes home, he'll put in a manager, and spend most of his time in London." She gave another watery sniff. "And what about Freddie and Jodear?"

"We've all hoped that those two would come together."

"Eliza, I spoke to Freddie about this and do you know what his reply was?" Indignation tinged the question.

"He said that he was as familiar to Jodear as the afternoon shadows on the barndoor. Oh!"

"Freddie is acting correctly Fanny, in not proposing to Jodear. Did you know that he had spoken to Joseph about Joanna and Joseph has given his permission to marry, if and when the time is ripe?"

Mrs. Linnett gathered the disconsolate figure close as she had done so many times in the past, handing Fanny a more substantial handkerchief and said bracingly, "We'll keep in touch. Perhaps we'll see you all coming out to Australia for a holiday. By then Jodear might have woken up."

"Yes, we could do that," replied Fanny and Mrs. Linnett was thankful that her friend's mercurial spirits had steadied.

"Now come, dear. We'll go and join our menfolk. Joseph has news that, I'm sure will delight you."

As the ladies went downstairs again Mrs. Linnett's thoughts were on the

82

weeks ahead. Everything they possessed would have to be packed; the voyage and how they would all fare; the children cooped up for months ahead. An involuntary shudder shook her body, but her face was serene as her eyes met her husband's worrying glance. She smiled across at him.

Adam had caught Fanny around the waist and with a joyful roar, lifted his small wife off her feet and danced around with her until she cried for mercy.

He sat her in her usual chair. "My love, I've purchased Jade Place for Freddie. Now, what do you think about that, eh?"

Fanny's face lightened, her hazel eyes sparkling, her hands clasped on her breast. "A lovely, lovely idea, dear Joseph and thank you, Adam."

"Well said, my love," plucking her once more out of her chair to dance once more around the room.

Watching these two dear people Eliza was comforted. The Squire had always been exactly what Fanny needed.

★ ★ ★

Freddie and Susan, the second daughter of the Martin family, had chosen the garden in which to discuss this momentous piece of news, taking with them Beth and Joanna. The move had been thoroughly thrashed out, Susan and Joanna remarking that it would be a glorious adventure. Only Beth and Freddie had reservations, Beth because it would mean never seeing Bertie again and Freddie because he was afraid of losing Joanna forever. This was almost more than he could bear, as he glanced at her with a rueful tenderness that she failed to see.

Freddie said with a puzzled air, merely as a change of subject. "Shocking news your father having to sell his business, but what I can't understand is why he never thought to place the new machinery in quite a different building,

84

with progressive workers who would be quite happy and willing to comply with the rules laid down."

"Evidently, from what Father told Mother, the few words Jed overheard, was that the new buyers are going to do just that," said Joanna.

"Jed, our listeningpost," murmured Susan. "How many times haven't we've heard news that we had no business to hear?"

"Pity Uncle Joseph didn't think of that before all that machinery was smashed," said Freddie sitting astride, as usual, on a tatty garden chair which had done sterling service over the years and was about to give up the ghost.

Beth plaiting lengths of grass looked up at him, sighed, said: "There wasn't enough money to get other premises. Did you know that Uncle Adam has bought Jade Place for you, dear Freddie. I'm so glad."

"Where on earth did you get that titbit from?" he asked sharply. "You're not pulling my leg, are you? Have I

85

missed something? My mind has been devilishly taken up with this move of yours but what a splendid piece of news — if it is true."

Joanna, who was sitting on the grass in a most unladylike fashion nodded. "Jed just happened to be in Father's outer office when this matter was being discussed with our lawyer."

"Jodear, will you be glad?" Freddie enquired. "I'll need a wife."

Joanna quite oblivious to any undercurrents replied blythly, "Freddie, it's the very nicest piece of news. I don't think any of us fancied the idea of strangers in Jade Place taking over our home and all our secret places, And a wife? Oh Freddie! Not yet, please. You're my very bestest dancing partner."

The younger fry were unanimous in their verdict that a trip to Australia was very much to their liking. The Martin section was frankly envious, Jed's word for it, splendiferous.

It was Beth who said that she for one,

would miss the loving ministrations of Aunt Fanny and Uncle Adam. "What other family are so blessed to have had two sets of parents?"

"Speak for yourself," muttered Freddie. "I got birched twice for the same misdeed, on several occasions."

Susan piped up. "We're all going to miss each other."

"Some more than others." This from Freddie.

"We'll all write every month," chipped in Joanna. "Promise?"

* * *

The days flew by. Mr. Linnett was kept busy going over the details of the business with the new owner, which left Mrs. Linnett having to make all the arrangements with Pickfords Removers to pack up the house. Their passage to Australia had been booked, Mr. Linnett having found it cheaper to go by sailing ship than by steam boat.

During the busy weeks that followed

Mrs. Linnett could not but help worrying what the future had in store for them all, when they finally reached their destination. It was no light undertaking to pull up all roots and take five children, the youngest being three months, to the other side of the world on a long and probably, tedious journey.

Her brothers were there, which would be a help, but were lax correspondents, so when the children and Nanny asked what they would take and what to throw out, she had no option but to say everything. "It will at least save us money if we don't have to buy goods when we get there."

One sunshiny afternoon Mrs. Linnett and her three daughters went shopping. She had promised that each of the girls could choose a dress length for themselves.

"Mother, I'll need some help to make my dress," lisped Lizzie prettily.

"Of course. Beth or Joanna will help," promised her mother, busy with her shopping list, so did not see the baleful glares from her other daughters who seethed at Lizzie's put on good behaviour, knowing full well that one of them would have to make the entire dress.

"My dears, I'm afraid we'll still have to make all our clothes until your father has established himself again," said Mrs. Linnett apologetically.

"Never mind, Mother," said Joanna, plumping herself down as John Coachman ceremoniously handed up his ladies into the carriage before driving off. "Perhaps we'll even open up a dressmaking establishment, call ourselves by some high falutin, nonsensical French name and charge exorbitant prices."

Beth continued in the same vein with more animation than she had shown for some time. "And we might even design a new style. We might even make our fortunes!"

Mrs. Linnett chuckled. "What a splendid idea and who knows, it might not be so very nonsensical as we think."

Lizzie reared herself up to say something scathing, caught Joanna's wicked glance and sank back again, sticking out her tongue, when her mother's head was turned.

"Nearly blotted your copybook that time," murmured Joanna.

For John Coachman this was a sentimental journey through the streets of London. If his eyes were a little blurred no one but himself was aware of it. Knowing his employer's situation, he'd been moved when he learned that he would be receiving a pension. He and his wife had already made plans to go to their daughter in Harrogate.

Mr. and Mrs. Swales would also be pensioned off and John knew that they too would be living with their eldest daughter, while the tweeny had been placed quite satisfactorily elsewhere.

Their first stop was a shop with A. Holmes Apothecary written in bold letters on the small window.

Mr. Holmes had sold medicines to the family for years and was sad when he heard that he would be losing their valued custom. He was most helpful when Mrs. Linnett asked him to advise her on which medicines to take to Australia.

"Hm, yes," looking over his spectacles at the well stocked shelves and began to take down various packets and bottles.

"Peruvian Bark, Cinnamon, Dover's Powder. I know about those," said Mrs. Linnett. "And that awful smelly stuff one mixes with lard to rub on to chests. Tartrametic, or something sounding like that. Spirits of camphor for colds and — I'll leave the rest to you, Mr. Holmes. I've brought my medicine chest, please fill it with whatever you think we'll need in a developing country. I'm afraid doctors will be few and far between." She turned as John brought in the box which was partitioned into small compartments of various sizes. Mrs. Linnett had been led to believe that these boxes were used by ships' doctors.

Joanna listening to all this, murmured to Beth. "It's sounds like an incantation to me, but Mother's idea of tying one of Father's smelly socks around our necks, plus rubbing on our chests that awful stuff, is bound to make us well quickly, if only to get rid of that smelly sock."

Mr. Holmes was most fulsome in his good wishes for the family and saw them to their carriage shaking his balding head which was surrounded by wisps of grey hair.

"Goodbye, Mr. Holmes," called out Joanna as the carriage rolled forward. "We'll miss coming in to buy your pennyworth of sweeties."

Mrs. Linnett sank back against the squabs with a sigh. "The haberdashers next, John."

The carriage turned into Bond Street.

London at its best, thought Mrs. Linnett nostalgically. I'm going to miss this dear city. The street was filled with an array of elegant, fashionably dressed ladies and gentlemen all taking a stroll in the bright afternoon sunshine.

Their stop at the haberdashers was short and then on to the mercers which stocked muslins, silks and velvets. It was here where they met Mrs. Blenkenthorpe and Edwina her eighteen year old daughter. A tall, very thin girl with a sharp pixie face and huge brown eyes which she used to good effect. At the first opportunity, she dragged Joanna over to see a particularly fine muslin in white with dainty, embroidered pink and mauve flowers.

Joanna immediately fell in love with it, determined to buy a length.

"Oh, never mind the material," said Edwina impatiently. "I wanted to talk to you. When do you leave for Australia?"

"In a couple of weeks time. Why."

"Oh, good."

Joanna's glance was puzzled. "Why so pleased?"

Edwina simpered which made Joanna long to shake her. "I'm hoping to make Freddie Martin my particular dancing partner and then, who knows?" with a toss of her black curls.

"Edwina, you goose. One does not choose a dancing partner. You should know that." Joanna wondered why the very thought of it was causing a ruffle of anger through her and was relieved when the assistant came across to take her order.

On the return journey she glanced anxiously at her mother. She looked so tired. Hoping to lift that weary look she said with a chuckle. "I've enjoyed the afternoon immensely, Mother. It was becoming very boring, all that packing. Beth became quite cross when I suggested we throw everything into the boxes. They'll all be creased anyway, by the time we reach our journey's end, no matter how tidily we pack."

She had the pleasure of seeing her mother smile and say, "My dears, we'll go upstairs and look into the trunks in the attic that haven't been opened for years and throw out what we don't require."

"But, Mother, we have already gone through those trunks." This from Lizzie. "These dresses we're wearing were made from old ones."

Beth suddenly sat up as they turned into their street. There was a carriage outside their house. "Who, I wonder can that be? Oh, it's Bertie." A strangled gasp came from her at this unexpected visitor and clasped her hands together until the knuckles stood out white.

"He asked if he could come and see you for the last time, Bethie," said her Mother and before she could go on, Beth caught her hand in hers.

"Please, please Mama, I — I'd rather not see him alone. I said my adieus at Lady Newton's dance. There is nothing more to say."

Mrs. Linnett patted her hand. "Very well, dear, we'll all go into the drawingroom. "Ah, Bertie," extending a

95

hand to the young man who helped her down. "Come inside. Come inside," and led the way into the hall where Swales met them. "Please bring in the tea as soon as possible."

★ ★ ★

Mrs. Linnett carried on a creditable conversation enquiring after Bertie's parents and what his future plans were, but nobody was very comfortable, even after the teatray had been brought in. Bertie soon took his leave, a little taken aback when Beth refused to go with him to the door and included her goodbyes along with the others.

★ ★ ★

As Mrs. Linnett left the drawingroom, her thoughts turned to Lizzie. She hadn't failed to notice the byplay between her daughters and could not banish her uneasy suspicions that Lizzie wasn't always the well behaved daughter she thought her to be. Mrs. Linnett sighed. She would look into this on board ship. There would be plenty of time and opportunity and relegated it to the back of her mind. It was time for baby Sarah's feed.

Meanwhile the three young ladies were having a merry hour in the school-room, taking out from the humped-back trunks, which had been brought down from the attic, all the old castoff clothes of years, holding them against themselves, giggling a great deal at the odd fashions they represented, the smell of camphor filling the air.

Beth had in her arms an amber silk gown, with yards in the skirt, hugging it to her. "Isn't this lovely," she breathed. "Worn over a hoop, of course."

"It would be a deuce of a nuisance when dancing," replied Joanna. "As Freddie would say," seeing Beth's disapproval. "That colour is perfect for you. That one must be kept." She had just unearthed a pair of trousers. "Wonder how Father ever managed to sit down," holding the garment against her.

"I believe they were knitted to adapt to a person's figure," but Beth had eyes only for the amber ball gown that had been worn by her mother.

"Look at this," giggled Lizzie, holding up a wire contraption. "What on earth is it?"

"Used for holding up a topless bodice. Thank goodness we don't have to wear them now," said Joanna her head in the trunk.

As the days passed, the house hummed like a swarm of angry bees. The big trunks littered the rooms and as they were filled taken into the stables. Tempers frayed.

The usually good tempered Mrs. Swales demanded to know what had happened to the bed linen that had been ironed at the beginning of the week. "It's that dratted Miss Lizzie," she raved. "I asked her to put it away. I've never known such a skitterwitted child in my life," and flounced from the room. It was left to Beth to sort that one out.

One early evening Mrs. Linnett and Beth slipped out of the house into the perfumed garden. A soft breeze ruffled the leaves of trees and shrubs and Mrs. Linnett lifted her head thankfully to its coolness. They strolled in companionable silence, past the wide border of nasturtiums, snapdragons and Canterbury bells, old friends that had been in the same spot for years — past roses romping over the stone walls. It was only now, with the knowledge of their move, that she etched the picture on her mind. So much taken for granted and a sadness filled her. How could she ever bear to leave this home of theirs?

They had reached the old sundial, standing in a round bed of pansies, with its motto. 'Time is, Time was, Time is not.'

Mrs. Linnett slipped a hand through Beth's arm. "I wonder where we'll be this time next year? Are you looking forward to the trip, Beth?"

"One place is as good as another, I suppose," she replied listlessly and Mrs. Linnett could feel her shrug.

"Dear, I just want to say how very much your father and I love and admire you. These last months have not been easy, but I've learnt that what cannot be cured, must be endured," and gave Beth's arm a loving squeeze.

Only Beth knew of the dragging inertia that had had to be fought that not even the packing or the prospect of a sea voyage had assuaged. Her disappointment at Bertie's unwillingness to stop his gambling for her sake, had subsided into a dull aching loss.

"There wasn't very much else I could have done, was there, Mother?"

"No, dear," she agreed as they made their way back to the house, adding sadly, "This dear England, will we ever see her again and baby Sarah will never know or love her homeland."

Later that same evening Freddie joined Joanna sitting under the great elm in Jade Place's garden. It had represented so many things in their childhoods' past. Pirate ship, King's Castle, or just a retreat in which to feel at peace with the world, hidden in its leafy coolness, with a red, juicy apple.

Would this tall beautiful girl ever become aware of his love for her? Does so much for my manly ego, Freddie thought wryly. Here in this evening light her face wore a rapt wonderment that she had never lost or outgrown when communing with nature.

He sat down beside her. His childhoods liking for this effervescent, lovable madcap had deepened with the years and yet he could not bring himself to tell her of this love he hid deep in his heart.

It was Joanna who broke their companionable silence.

"I'm so glad that you'll own Jade Place, Freddie dear. Now there will be no hurt, no sorrow when we leave this dear place."

"I'm going to miss you very much, Jodear. You know that don't you?"

She nodded turning to him. "Wish you were coming too. That would make everything perfect," but there was only friendly regret in her words.

Freddie grinned. "Many a word said in jest and all that. Father has already tentatively suggested that to Mother, but she wasn't impressed."

A flight of crows making their raucous way home broke the spell. Joanna rose to her feet. "I must be going in. Freddie, don't you think this move will be a splendid adventure?"

"No! It's going to be damned lonely without you."

After weeks of frantic activity, the day eventually arrived when all the packing had been completed and Pickfords Flying Wagons were at the door. In a short space of time the house was denuded of everything movable and the wagons left for the wharf.

Certain items of furniture and trunks were to go into the cabins allotted to the family, the rest into stowage. Mrs. Linnett devoutly hoped that her orders would be carried out correctly.

She need not have worried, however, for Pickfords had an excellent reputation for prompt delivery and excellent service.

There were tearful farewells when the family bade goodbye to the Swales, Esmerelda, the tweeny and John Coachman, although John would be driving them to the wharf later that afternoon.

For the last time Mrs. Linnett toured the now empty rooms. The house was no longer hers, she had no right to be here. Her throat closed with tears she tried to hold back, as she quietly closed each door on the numerous memories that sprang to mind and as she went downstairs her fingers trailed lovingly down the bannisters. Joseph was waiting for her in the hall.

"'Home is where the heart is' my dear," he reminded her gently. "Bless you, you are a great homemaker, Eliza," and held her close for a second. Taking her arm, he led her outside, locking the front door for the last time.

The whole family had elected to walk over to the Martins' house where they were to have luncheon.

Beth's hand crept into her mother's. "We were happy in Jade Place and that is why it is such a wrench to leave," she murmured with a wisdom of her nineteen years.

Mrs. Linnett nodded. "And everyone has been so kind and helpful. Even folk that we don't know so well and — " She broke off, her voice totally suspended by tears, but by the time the family reached the house she had herself well under control, her smile though, was a travesty of the real thing. Not that Fanny's was much better.

As they had approached the Martins house, Beth, with a deep sense of the inevitable realised, with almost a sense of shock, that they would never again see this lovely, old property, with its steeply gabled roof and massive front door and attendant solid brass knocker which had always been open to the Linnett family; remembered the numerous games of hopscotch played on the black and white marble squares in the hall; the schoolroom where they all had been tutored in alternate years. This scheme had been advantageous as only one tutor had been necessary for both families. Later the older children had studied with the rector, who was a notable Latin and Greek scholar. Jed was the only one who had attended of late.

Luncheon was a strangely silent meal. After all everything that had to be said had been chewed over and over again. Everyone was relieved when the time came for the arrival of the carriages that were to take them to the port. The Martins had insisted that they would say their final farewells there.

John Coachman stood by the carriage for the last time. His usual cheerful countenance forbidding in its sorrow. He opened the door and let down the steps, the varnish and brass shining. Ceremoniously he handed in his ladies.

Mr. Linnett paused and wrung John's hand. "I make you a present of this coach and the horses. Thank you for your faithful service to this family. Bless you, John."

The old coachman, for a moment was struck dumb. "Sir!" not quite believing his aging ears. "Sir, but you have already given me a pension." Then eagerly. "Do you think I might start up a small business by taking people here and there?" he quavered ecstatically.

"An excellent idea, John. Give you something to do and get you out from under your wife's feet," wringing his old retainer's hand again.

They passed Jade Place for the last time, Mrs. Linnett's heart sore within her. No more would she be mistress of the house; no more would she witness the sun kissing out the crocuses that starred the back garden. Would there be these lovely flowers on the other side of the world?

Mr. Linnett took her hand in his. Please God may I be doing the right thing, he thought to himself. In their luggage was one new fabric printing machine that had not been wrecked along with the others, for the simple reason that it had not been unpacked and felt his spirits soar.

"My love, we'll easily be able to start up again, just you wait and see."

"Yes, dear," murmured his wife dutifully.

The countryside was beautiful. It was a good summer, with cornfields just beginning to gold and orchards flying their colours amid stands of green trees.

John was slowing down to turn into the harbour area, then stopped.

It was a tearful farewell as the family said their goodbyes to the old man, the children hugging and kissing him.

"Wishing you were coming, John," piped up Jed. "No doubt we'll be needing a coachman in Australia."

"Not me, Master Jed. Not at my age. God go with you all," and drove away.

Douglas and his wife were waiting on the wharf, she being big with child. Eva was a petite blonde, with huge blue eyes and a happy smile.

Mrs. Linnett held her daughter-in-law in a convulsive embrace.

"Oh, my dear, we won't see our grandchild. May all go well with you and the little one."

"Perhaps you will be seeing us, Mother Linnett. Who knows? If you all like Australia, we might come for a visit."

Mrs. Linnett suddenly brightened. "Douglas dear, have you been discussing this?"

"Mama, yes," and put an arm around his mother, "but only vaguely. We wouldn't emigrate. Eva would be too far from her family. We'll miss you all, though. It just won't seem the same without you."

"Hope you'll be happy with the new owners," said his father gruffly.

"Up to the present, we're on very agreeable terms. Please don't worry."

"Oh, look," interrupted Lizzie. "All the boats are like trees in winter, awaiting the Spring."

The tension eased, Mr. Linnett smiling at the simile. "Well, my dear, our ship will be blossoming with the tide."

There before them lay the huge sailingship *The Barberos* peacefully at anchor in the Port of London, swaying to the lap of water against the harbour wall. A great deal of activity was going on, as dock hands loaded the ship with cargoes destined for ports in Africa and Australia. Sailors were scurrying around getting the ship ready to sail on the afternoon tide. The children were fascinated.

It was a silent group of grownups,

though, who waited for the call to embark. Feelings were running too high for any social chitchat. It was Jed who provided welcome relief when he asked his father if he could take Gyp along. He had had second thoughts about smuggling the dog aboard, his conscious pricking him to an unnatural degree.

"I — I suppose Freddie would look after him," he gulped. "But — but Gyp would be a real asset in Australia, Father," he added hopefully, his grey eyes pleading.

Mr. Linnett gave his son a startled stare, suddenly realising what a singularly imperceptient parent he had become. Busy all day at his place of business, he had had little time to devote to the upbringing of his children. Shame swept through him. "I did not notice Gyp in either of the carriages. I suppose you had him under your coat?"

Jed shook his head. "I travelled in the Martins' carriage, Sir."

The Squire chuckled.

Mr. Linnett's glance was following the line of the wharf. "It's not for me to say, Jed. You will have to apply to the Captain. I think that is he coming this way. By the bye, his name is Captain Blyth."

"Bet you a pea to a pound," prophesied Mr. Martin, "that Jed will wind that gentleman around his grubby little finger."

Once again the tension had been eased, Jed paying scant heed to this animadversion as he watched the imposing figure bear down upon them. Captain Blyth was huge, white whiskered and round of face that had been fissured and burnt brown by the weather of the tropics. His black morning coat was richly embellished with gold braided epaulettes and on his head a hat that appeared incongruous atop his bulk.

He shook Mr. Linnett by the hand and was introduced to the two families and as he turned away Jed approached him a little uncertainly, Gyp held tight against his chest, his calflick lending a comical air to his face.

"Sir! Are you the Captain?" awe in his voice.

"I am that, Sonny. Are you a passenger or a spectator come to say farewell?" The fierce brown eyes beetled over boy and the dog. "Hmm?"

"I'm a passenger, Sir, but Gyp here is a spectator. Could he also become a passenger, do you think? He is an excellent ratter. I — I'll share my dinner with him," he suggested hopefully, meeting the fierce gaze steadily, his manner propriety itself. "I'll miss him so much, Sir, I'll never see him again. Do you think, Sir — " The words were allowed to hang in mid air, his expression saying the rest.

Everyone looked on in amusement as Jed wheedled around the Captain. They all knew, sometimes to their cost, how persuasive he could be in times of need.

"Humph!" snorted the Captain. "So

that dog isn't on my passenger list, hmm?" smiling down at Jed and running a finger down his nose. "I could include that misbegotten hound on the crew sheets as — as chief ratcatcher."

Jed beamed. "Oh, thank you, Sir."

The Captain continued, stabbing a stubby finger on Jed's chest. "You will at all times be personally responsible for that dog; you will scrub the deck if he fouls it, or else I'll have your head for washing, my lad."

Jed was nodding madly, a wide grin splitting his face. "You're a great gun, Sir."

"Ha!" a frown adding to the lines on the Captain's face, as if something had just struck him. "Where do you think he'll do his business?"

Jed looked blank.

"Oh, never mind that now. Have to think of far more important matters," said Captain Blyth testily. "Ladies and gentlemen, only another ten minutes, please. It will be hightide within the hour and I'm sure you'd like to inspect your cabins and straighten yourselves out before we sail."

With that he strode off, but as he approached the gangway, he turned and said with a scowl. "Lad, you could always hold that animal over the side."

There was much hugging and kissing. Even the children suddenly found lumps in their throats, making words gruff and unnatural. The Squire blew his nose fiercely, his shaggy eyebrows working as he tried to keep his emotions under control. Mrs. Linnett and Mrs. Martin wept openly.

Freddie managed to draw Joanna aside. "I'm going to miss you sorely. When the trees turn to Autumn and I rob the hives of their honey, I'll remember the colour of your hair, Jodear. You've always been part of the Martin family, part of me. Don't forget, Jodear, please."

His gaze was so intent, hoping to embed her face in his memory, afraid that the years would bring forgetfulness, that her eyes flew to his. The urgency in his voice was so unlike him.

"I'll miss you, funnyface," was all he could find to say.

There was still no trace of awareness in her candid, beautiful deep blue eyes. She had not perceived what he was trying to convey to her. He couldn't be plainer.

"You are so — and I'm — oh! There is so much I'd like to say. Dash it all! Was ever a man in such a coil?" his hands going to her shoulders and with a rueful, tender smile, Freddie bent down and lightly placed a feather kiss on her lips. "Just a farewell gift, Jodear. A gift of friendship to a longstanding, very dear girl."

She nodded mutely. Mrs. Martin took her son's place and gathered Joanna into her ample embrace. "God bless you, my dear," she murmured tearfully.

"Last call, ladies and gentlemen, please." The Captain's personal servant had come up to them. "Just call me Mac."

He was a funny little man who wore his wine-coloured jacket, fawn waistcoat and trousers with a decided air of a gentleman's gentleman, as he shepherded his charges up the gangway.

Nanny, whose hat held no less than five hatpins, was clutching her over large handbag to her chest, found herself being hustled along, much to her annoyance.

Mrs. Linnett followed her, carrying baby Sarah, Joseph the last to embark.

"Hope you are taking the right children, for don't ask me who's who," quipped the Squire.

The last words were for Freddie. Mr. Linnett shook his hand, shocked at the rawness of his expression. "I'll keep you informed, dear fellow," he said quietly. "Will post a letter from the Cape of Good Hope," and was pleased to see a lessening of the pain.

"Will you, indeed, Sir? Thank you," and wrung Mr. Linnett's hand. His blame. Why hadn't he proposed to Joanna and taken his chance? No, no! He smiled crookedly as he followed his family to their carriage, wondering if there would ever be a chance for him to plan a trip to Australia.

3

IT had been decided that the Martin family would not linger to wait for the ship to sail, so Mr. and Mrs. Linnett and Nanny after a wave from the deck went to inspect their accommodation which they found to be most adequate.

Mrs. Linnett thankfully took off her bonnet and coat, patted her sable hair, that showed only a trace of grey in its luxuriant depths.

Nanny was bustling about the cabin.

"Sit down, Madam and rest quietly. Sarah needs a feed. Bless her, so good she has been. Here, let me help you off with your dress. Your wrapper is on the top of this case."

"Dear Nanny, what would we do without you? Even the footstool is here."

Nanny handed over the baby and

a blessed calm reigned in the cabin though there was still a considerable bustle on deck and on the quayside.

The children were still hanging over the rails, waving their handkerchiefs until all the Martin family had disappeared from sight. There was also, more than enough activity going on to hold their interest.

Sailors with gold earrings were being hustled by an exasperated officer yelling blasphemous, furious, expletives, while the Captain roared out his orders from the bridge.

Jed grinned, the quivering, excited dog caught in a tight embrace. He murmured to Beth. "Wonder how the parents and Nanny are going to react to this kind of language?"

"I'm shocked myself, but we'll just have to accept. It's going to be an awfully long journey."

"We're moving," shouted Jed as the buildings began to slide gently away. "Wonder if any of us will ever see our homeland again?"

Joanna, a little apart was astonished how bereft she suddenly felt as the Martins' carriage faded into the distance. The realisation that she would never see Freddie again hit her and had to open wide her eyes to allow the teardrops to drain back. What was wrong with her. She never cried, well, not in public. Tears were private as was that kiss Freddie had given her. Freddie had kissed her? Her very first grownup kiss. Outrage should have been her first reaction, instead her fingers went involuntarily to her lips.

The harbour was soon left behind, the sails fed with a drive-force wind, spray flying up as the bow sliced a way through the ocean.

The children continued to hang over the rails and joined in the shouting and waving of sailors and harbour workers on the outer wall, then made their way quickly up the companionway to the Quarterdeck where the cabins were situated, laughing and holding on to each other, a little unsure of the heaving planks beneath their very unsure feet.

They found their parents moving their furniture around, Sarah peacefully asleep in her crib, thumb in mouth. Nanny was unpacking.

"Why, this is all our own furniture," cried Jed, his mouth agape. "It's just like home, or nearly so," catching his father's sardonic glance. "Even your own bed. And that's the rosewood table that was in the hall in Jade Place."

"Where are we all to sleep?" Lizzie wanted to know.

Her father replied that Beth and Joanna would share the next cabin, Nanny, Sarah and Lizzie the one after that and Jed the cubbyhole further down.

Pickfords had done their job well and beyond the fact of having to shift some items around, the furniture was in the right cabins.

"We can't have that chest of drawers over there," were the first words from

Joanna as she and Beth entered their cabin.

"It will be too heavy to shift. I'll go and find a sailor," and Beth flew outside again and noticed a well dressed gentleman approaching.

He was tall and strongly built; coat of bottlegreen accompanying fawn trousers and a plain cream shirt, but she decided that his face was far too austere for her liking. His grey-green eyes gemlike and as cold; his hair sunbleached above flyaway brows. Here was no sailor and judged him to be in his late twenties.

"Good-day, Sir. My sister and I need some help in moving an item of furniture. Could you — " drawing back at his frown, his eyes holding a distinctly hostile expression. "I — I wasn't aware that there were other passengers. Pray forgive me. Who are you?" curiosity getting the better of her.

"Perhaps your doctor?" His well modulated voice was cynical.

Beth blinked, taken aback by his abrupt manner. She bristled. "Ah, the ship's doctor, I presume and a law unto yourself, no doubt?"

The man bowed. "I haven't the time now to discuss my status, Ma'am."

"Well, don't let me keep you, Sir. I never expected you to help me," she replied indignantly. "A sailor is whom we require."

"I'll have someone sent up," and walked off, perfectly at ease on the rolling deck.

Beth watched him disappear down the companionway and retraced her steps, put out by his behaviour and a little on edge. Nobody had ever had this effect of making her act so pertly. She smiled as she realised that she had enjoyed the altercation, finding it most stimulating, but did wonder why the gentleman had looked so forbidding. In future I'll no more be a mouse to say aye and amen to everything, she decided firmly.

"I've just met the ship's doctor and

what a rude man he is," Beth said to Joanna entering their cabin again and told her all that had transpired. "And what is more, Jodear, I don't know whether he'll ask a sailor to come and help us or not. He didn't greet me or introduce himself." Her sense of grievance was still very evident.

"Beth, there was nobody to introduce you," teased Joanna with a smile. "I've never seen your feathers ruffled this badly before. Your cheeks are quite pink and your eyes are sparkling."

Beth sat down abruptly before the dressing-table mirror. Her cheeks glowed attractively and stormy eyes met her glance and at that sight, her laughter bubbled out. "Oh, dear, I don't know what came over me," and turned around at the knock on the door.

There stood a burly sailor, rough of face, but kindly. What was more, he was quite willing to do their bidding.

In a very short space of time, the cabin was to the ladies' liking and Joanna suggested that he go along to each of the cabins to see if he could be of some further use.

"Well," said Beth kneeling beside a big trunk, "that was soon done and here is the bed linen. The blankets must be in those canvas bags over there. Pickfords have been most efficient."

"How nice to have our own furniture," said Joanna, seating herself in the easy chair, after the beds had been made, but Beth would not allow this.

"Come along. We'll go and help the others."

★ ★ ★

Jonathan Barber, the ship's doctor, leaning against the ship's railing, enjoying the cool late afternoon air was meditating, unhappily, on the day's unexpected turn of events. Passengers on *The Barberos*?

Captain Blyth when he had said goodbye after the last trip, had not been contemplating passengers. Such a large anchor as the Linnett family,

125

plus a nanny, dropped into the small pond of their existence on the ship, was likely to make something of a splash.

He strode purposefully up the companionway to the Quarterdeck where the Captain's suite was situated and entered the well appointed cabin.

The Captain, relieved of his duties, welcomed him, waving to a chair.

"You're looking rattled, Jonathan," pouring the doctor a drink. "Something bothering you?"

"It's the passengers, Sir. You never mentioned, after the last trip, that you were thinking along these lines," his voice accusing. "What made you change your mind?"

Captain Blyth, with a glass in his hand made himself more comfortable in his vast, sagging chair. "My granddaughter, Emmy, cheeky little rascal," this with a fond chuckle, "accused me of being just like Captain Wentworth in Miss Austin's *Persuasion* and quoted her very words. 'No ship under my command, shall ever convey a family of ladies anywhere, if I can help it,' and then, ' — women and children have no right to be comfortable on board.' What do you think about that? And then Tom, my son, persuaded me that a few passengers would be company on the long voyages. I liked the idea," with a quizzical stare at his doctor.

"I met Mr. Linnett, a gentleman, with three daughters, a son and a baby of four months. When I met them all earlier this afternoon they seemed a delightful family. I'm looking forward to this trip enormously. Hmm!" seeing the sceptical glance flung at him. "You'll still have your old cabin, dear boy."

"Not demoted to the stowage, Sir?"

"Have you met any of the passengers yet?" asked the Captain carefully.

"Only a very young lady — "

"What did you think of her?"

"She has the most beautifully defined eyebrows I've ever seen. They look as if they had been etched by a master hand.

I expect they are artificial."

"Didn't you notice anything else about her?"

"No."

"I did this really for you, Jonathan. Thought you might appreciate feminine company for a while." An impish smile creased the craggy face.

"And Sir, I'll remind you that from now on you will have to have a haircut frequently. I've seen that white thatch of yours sticking out from under your cap like stubble beneath a nesting bird," retorted the doctor acidly. "And, what is more a certain young lady on this ship is demanding good manners from us all. That includes you, Captain."

He chuckled as Jonathan left, slamming the door behind him. Sitting back in his easy chair again, Captain Blyth recalled the frank, open, young man of three and twenty, with his easy, yet unassuming manners who had signed on as the doctor on *The Barberos* for a short trip to the

Isles north of England and compared that memory with Jonathan Barber as he was today. He shook his head sadly. His innate good manners to himself remained, but the openness had vanished. The barriers had been up for far too long.

When Jonathan had first signed on he had been about to marry a very pretty girl called Marla. Several trips later, he had again applied for the berth of doctor on *The Barberos*, a changed man. All the Captain had been able to find out from him was that the wedding had not taken place. They were not suited.

The Captain shook off his uneasy thoughts and chuckled. Those two bonny lasses of Mr. Linnett's should change the old grouse.

★ ★ ★

Later that evening Mr. and Mrs. Linnett and the two eldest girls were to dine with the Captain as he was desirous of making their acquaintance and also to introduce them to his officers.

Beth and Joanna had just finished their toilettes when Nanny bustled in to fuss over them both, running a comb down Joanna's wayward fringe and straightening Beth's sash that matched her primrose gown.

Nanny, a privileged person, could say to Beth, "Please wear a smile tonight, my dear. I realise it's not the happiest of days for you, but the Captain does deserve a pleasant guest." She stood back and studied her charges. "You are both lovely."

Both girls hugged her promising to tell her all about everything in the morning.

The moon was coming down a path of velvet as the family made their way to the Captain's suite, where they were ushered in by Mac, the Captain's personal valet, who bowed and led them into a surprisingly spacious saloon, woodpanelled, with long ruby-red cushioned seats running along two sides.

Mrs. Linnett's eyes widened as she took in the beautiful oak diningroom suite at the other end of the saloon; the well-appointed table with its snowy napery and silver cutlery. There was also a bookcase, glass-fronted. Mr. Linnett's eyes gleamed, longing to go over to it and learn its contents.

The family were introduced to the second in command, one Herbert Bradford and the junior officer William Willett, both young presentable men. Both in uniform.

Beth's eyes fell as the third man was introduced. He was the man whom she had met earlier on and was, indeed, the ship's doctor. There was no sign of recognition in Jonathan Barber's casual glance as he bowed, murmured politely and turned to her father. His black coat and trousers, snowy white ruffled shirt were in impeccable taste, with no hint of the extravagances of prevailing fashions. She also noticed his well-shaped hands.

Beth and Joanna were looking particularly fetching in their summer muslins, with broad satin sashes, with silk flowers in their hair.

The Captain, somewhat overcome by all this beauty, rose ponderously to his feet, a glass in his hand. "To the ladies. God bless 'em. This is the first time *The Barberos* has entertained the fairer sex at our table. Welcome, welcome."

"Captain, I find it most interesting that we are the first passengers you have had on board. An experiment?" asked Mrs. Linnett who was sitting next to him at the dining table.

"Yes indeed, Ma'am and to my thinking this trip is going to be quite delightful."

The meal was a merry one, Joanna sitting on one side of the Captain and between her and Beth was Herbert Bradford, a rather thickset young man, who was delighted to welcome the two young ladies. He kept them well entertained with sea stories.

At the other end of the table sat Mr. Linnett with the doctor next to him. They immediately discovered kindred interests, both having a love of literature. William Willett, who Mrs. Linnett found to be a shy young man, was amused to see that his gaze often strayed in Beth's direction. Perhaps her daughter would be able to forget Bertie. She fervently hoped so.

After the meal which had been served by Mac, the guests were again led to the easy chairs on the other side of the spacious saloon.

The doctor went up the Mrs. Linnett and very correctly, offered her his services if the need arose. On the occasions when his eyes met Beth's, he noticed, with a twitch of his lips that she was very much on her dignity and wrote her off as a very young Miss.

To all this the Captain was an interested spectator, enjoying watching his quests. He had caught the glances his Junior Officer had directed at Miss Beth, looking so demure and pretty and now seated beside her. Bradford, if he wasn't mistaken, was much struck by Miss Joanna and who wouldn't be, he thought appreciatively. Her hair, caught up from each side of her face, was a mane of chestnut cascading down her back.

Who would have thought of all the amusement and pleasure a few passengers could bring and settled his vast bulk more comfortably in his chair.

"Miss Linnett, this is indeed a pleasure to have passengers on *The Barberos*. So glad you're here," this from Mr. Bradford, with an admiring glance. "Hope the Captain, bless him, will continue the practice."

"To ease your boredom, Mr. Bradford?"

"Oh, I say! Didn't mean it that way," and Joanna chuckled at his sheepish expression.

Meanwhile, Mr. Willett was saying something similar to Beth who was rapidly putting him at ease.

"May I say that it is a lovely surprise

to be privileged to entertain so lovely a lady at the Captain's table? We have never carried passengers before."

Beth was surprised. "Do you mean to say that the Captain has never taken passengers before? Why ever not?"

Mr. Willett shook his dark brown head, his eyes twinkling attractively. "Just one of those things, I suppose."

"Is the Captain a misogynist?"

"No! No! He has a large family and is a grandfather, quite a few times over, but passengers on *The Barberos*! What a turnup for the books," and lifted his eyebrows expressively. "What a trip this is going to be!" thus echoing the Captain's sentiments.

The doctor reviewing the evening as he made his last visit to the sickbay, thought that Bradford and Willett were much taken with the young ladies, in which case they would be more than happy to entertain them, leaving him free to get on with his work.

The hour was late when the Linnett family made their unsteady way back

135

to their cabins, clutching the rail of the Quarterdeck as the wind was boisterous as were the waves.

"We all appear to be good sailors," shouted Mrs. Linnett as she laughingly held on to her skirts.

"A very pleasant evening," added Mr. Linnett and both said goodnight to their daughters.

Beth and Joanna entered their cabin glad to be out of the wind. The lamp swayed gently with the roll of the ship, casting eerie shadows.

"I thought your doctor had very good manners," said Joanna, preparing for bed. "And a very personable man."

"Well, I did not appreciate his brusqueness this afternoon. And he's not my doctor."

Joanna yawned and pulled up the blanket. "He's probably had to leave a wife and children behind."

"Yes, I suppose so. Poor things," said Beth with ready sympathy. "How awful, but that is no excuse for bad manners."

Joanna nearly asleep. "Probably had other things on his mind. First day at sea. The other two men I found interesting. All those sea stories — "

Beth, however, lay awake. A sailor, somewhere, was playing a flute. A melody incredibly, hauntingly, sad. Someone had left a loved one behind.

"Oh, Bertie," she mourned and cried herself to sleep.

★ ★ ★

The Captain was very conscious of his passengers' comfort and advised them of the best areas where they could enjoy most the cooling breezes and where to place baby Sarah's crib, for it was becoming much warmer. Poor little dear, how uncomfortable it must be for her, he would think. A fleeting regret feathered his heart, that he was unable to enjoy more of his own grandchildren, but he was a man of the sea. Hopefully, one of his grandchildren would follow in his footsteps, making the sea his career.

As the days passed, Jed quickly edged his way into the Captain's heart, first of all by the meticulous reporting of the rats caught by Gyp and his keen thirst for knowledge, earning the Captain's respect. When Jed asked if he might be allowed to learn something about sailing, the Captain agreed and called a sailor to him.

"Take this nipper and show him the ropes. I'll break every bone in your body if even a hair of his head is ruffled."

The man nodded with a grin, showing his broken teeth. "Aye, aye, Captain, Sir," with a touch of his forelock.

Turning to Jed he said, "Spit on that there calflick, lad and come wif me."

Jed from then on had eyes that were never still, as they ran along the horizon, along the sheets and braces, learning what it was to be caught in a white squall, could talk intelligently about topsails and compass cards and pick out a badly trimmed sail.

The fairly good weather they had enjoyed did not continue; it was not to be expected.

Beth and Joanna were awoken early one morning to see their shoes and small cases sliding from one end of their cabin to the other. The sea was riding high. A warning came from the Captain to stay in their cabins. Low sullen black clouds rolled about the heavens accompanied by deafening claps of thunder and cracks of lightning. Peal after peal reverberated around the heavens and the family were quite happy to obey the Captain's command, except Jed, who would have dearly liked to have been on deck.

The storm became so bad that the two young ladies and Jed, who had dashed into their cabin for company, feared that the ship would turn turtle and stayed in their beds, heads under the covers. The lamp swung violently, items on the dressing-table had long since slid off the edge. Jed, in disgust went along to his parents' cabin and the girls hoped that was where he was going.

It was claustrophobia that eventually drove Beth out of the cabin as well. If they were to go down she'd rather be on the deck. Joanna wailed that the very idea made her stomach heave.

Beth dressed, adding a heavy cloak, imprisoning her hair in a scarf. As she stepped out on to the deck, the wind hit her, but hanging grimly on to the rail, she managed to reach a familiar nook, to sink thankfully down in its shelter.

It was bottomlessly dark beyond the eerie light of the lanterns, the ship being tossed about like a cockleshell, but Beth was so spellbound by the wonder and awesomeness of it all, that she had no thought as to her safety. Mountainous waves were breaking over the bow causing the vessel to shudder convulsively. Sailors scurried about like drunken men, their voices lost in the shriek of the wind through the rigging.

It was if some primeval force had taken Beth over and was only brought down to earth when a strong hand grabbed her shoulder and shook her.

A furious voice in her ear yelled. "Are you completely mad?"

Beth turned and recognised the doctor. He was up to his eyes in oilskins. Their eyes met and held, his brilliant with anger.

"Good-day to you, Doctor," her voice a high treble.

"What's good about it," he growled, shaking her even harder. "You could have been washed overboard," and put an arm around her.

"It costs nothing to be polite," retorted Beth.

"In any given situation." He suddenly laughed, five years falling from his face. "Polite to the very end."

"I'm enjoying this," she shouted back, the wind taking the words.

"So am I and you do appear to be a good sailor."

A particularly fierce gust made the

doctor tighten his hold.

"You're such a little thing, this gale will take you as easily as spindrift."

Beth was unconscious of the fact that with her fair hair escaping in curls from her scarf and her clear skin glowing against her dark cloak, she was beautiful.

The doctor gave her another shake. "Miss Linnett you will now return to your cabin. No, no," he added seeing her mouth open, "this isn't an order. It's just a suggestion. Come along, I'll take you back."

Beth found herself grateful for his strong arm as he helped her battle against the buffeting gale. She would never have managed on her own.

Joanna raised her head as Beth entered the cabin. She looked ghastly and Beth went quickly to her.

"Oh, my poor dear!"

"Thank goodness, you're back! I hate this ship. I hate — O — oh!" pressing a handkerchief to her mouth. Gratefully she took the basin held out to her.

Jed, at this inappropriate moment entered and had difficulty in closing the door again.

"Phew! What a gale! Great fun!"

"Are the rest of the family all right?" asked Beth anxiously.

"Yes, only Nanny is a little under the weather. Not that she'll ever admit it. They're all in the parents' cabin, with Gyp. I've come to see how you two are doing." He gave Joanna a considering glance. "Cast up your accounts, have you? That's the ticket. You'll feel much better now in a brace of shakes. Bound to," his eyes, momentarily, going to the basin.

"Go away, you horrid boy," she moaned. "I hate you, Jed."

He grinned. "First time I've ever seen Jodear ill," making for the door.

"Where are you going," asked Beth in alarm.

"Just out and about."

"The Captain said — " but Jed was gone.

Later Beth had the satisfaction of

seeing her sister drop off into a deep sleep.

★ ★ ★

By and large, the family had settled down very well to their new life. It helped having their own furniture in the cabins, down to the hip bath, jugs and basins on each wash stand, even the flower-patterned soap bowls. Dear familiar items.

There were certain chores that had to be done. Their cabins they cleaned themselves and did all the laundry. Meals were served in Mr. and Mrs. Linnett's cabin, where a large table had been provided, but there was still time to read, time for the children, time to relax.

The Captain again invited the family to dine with him. It had been at the suggestion of Herbert Bradford that the Captain provide some form of entertainment for his passengers. If the second in command had other reasons, he kept them to himself.

The evening provided several pleasures, of which music played the greater part. Beth was prevailed to play on the small, upright piano and Joanna to sing. The doctor was found to have a good tenor voice and turned the music score for Beth.

Once again Herbert paired off with Joanna and Willy with Beth. The Captain, with a fresh haircut, ignored Jonathan's amused smile and was quite content to entertain Mrs. Linnett, whom he found shared the same relatives somewhere amongst their ancestors, both being Devon born.

Later that evening, the doctor, in his very comfortable cabin sat at his desk, entering up his day's work, but try as he would, his mind kept wandering from the task on hand, to the memory of an enchanting little person, who had, in no uncertain terms, showed what she thought of his bad manners and the lovely smile she had bestowed upon Mr. Willett at the Captain's dinner party.

Well, what were lovely smiles, anyway, he thought cynically. Marla had had just such a lovely smile. Now he could please himself. He had no need to take a wife, his eldest brother, hale and hearty had sired two sons, which left him free from any family obligations.

Slipping off his silk dressing robe, he turned down the two lamps and climbed into his comfortable bed. No bunk for him, but the memory of Beth would not leave him, his professional interest aroused. Had the fact of emigrating been contrary to her wishes, having to leave a particular friend behind? Was it this that was making her so listless?

No answer came and as he closed his eyes, it was not Beth who came to mind, but Marla, whom he hadn't thought of for years. His dreams that night were not happy.

* * *

Halycon days sped by, the girls often seeing the doctor hurrying off somewhere, usually in his white smock which he used for surgery.

Mrs. Linnett had had to call him in to see Sarah. The baby had been very fretful and Nanny and Mrs. Linnett were at their wits' end. He had been so kind and understanding, handling the little one very expertly.

"Leave off some of her clothing, Nanny," he had advised. "She's only feeling the heat. Nothing to worry about, Mrs. Linnett. Sarah is very healthy."

He met Beth and Joanna coming up the companionway.

"Well! He at least raised his hat to us," remarked Beth.

"You've really got your dander up, haven't you? So unusual!"

"I've never disliked a person so much. Oh!" words failing her.

Joanna hid a smile. This distraction was just what her sister required. Wasn't this defiant, rebellious mood

147

against the doctor, perhaps the aftermath of her father's refusal to entertain Bertie's suit? Beth had been a dutiful daughter and an obedient one. Suddenly Joanna found herself intrigued and came out of her reverie when Beth said, "I must go. I promised Nanny to watch Sarah for a while, as she has a headache."

She fetched the baby and with a blanket walked to a shady nook just outside their cabin. Baby Sarah was rapidly becoming mobile.

This was where the doctor found her some time later and sat down on a corner of the blanket.

"Why are you so unhappy, Miss Linnett? Left a young man behind you? Hmm? You'll soon get over it," his tone indifferent, his gaze travelling, deliberately, over her delicate features.

"Sir!" Beth looked away quickly, furious at the rising tide of colour in her cheeks, leaving her defenceless.

"I'm your doctor. My glance was purely professional. Your health is also my concern. You are far too listless, on occasions when you think you are unnoticed. I am just wondering why?"

"It's got nothing to do with you, Doctor Barber. Your manners, as far as I'm concerned are not *comme il faut*. What are you doing now?"

The doctor had picked up Sarah and was taking off her dress, then her petticoat, leaving only a vest and nappy.

"There, more comfortable?" and hugged the fat little body to him.

Beth gaped. "What will Mother and Nanny say?"

"I've already told them to leave off some of her clothing. She'll be far happier now. Infants, in this weather, are subject to heat rash. Most uncomfortable."

"Oh," was all Beth could say.

"And you too, Miss Beth. You would be far more comfortable if you left off a few petticoats and suchlike," leaving her speechless, mouth dropped, face poppy-red.

"Well!"

When this piece of impertinence was relayed to Joanna, she chuckled and admitted that she for one was going to take Doctor Jonathan's advice. "Think of all the washing we'll save ourselves."

★ ★ ★

"You'll never get Nanny to part with any of her garments," retorted Beth and they laughed. "I still hold to the opinion that he has the most atrocious manners. He — he's too overpowering. Too — too — "

"Mature? Bertie was never that, Bethie." Joanna said gently. "That was his trouble." She sighed. "And what about Lizzie's manners? These worry me."

"Yes," agreed Beth, "but what can we do?"

"If someone doesn't correct that nasty nature, she'll never rule with her heart."

"Is that such a bad thing?"

"Now don't get bitter, Beth. It

150

doesn't suit you."

It was the following morning that Lizzie herself, brought down her mother's displeasure on to her own head.

She was lounging on her bed, Nanny and Sarah elsewhere, when Joanna marched into the room.

"What are you doing here?" she asked.

"Watching the motes floating on that sunbeam over there," with an airy wave of her hand.

"There can't be any motes. All the blankets were washed before we packed them. You're supposed to be helping with the washing."

"Yes, but it's so boring and, beside, my hands get all crinkly. Someone will do it for me, I expect."

Joanna swooped down and pulled Lizzie off the bed on to the floor.

"You beast, you beast! I'll tell Mother — " Her words trailed off as she became conscious of who was standing in the doorway. Her mother looked most severe.

Lizzie hurriedly scrambled to her feet, her eyes wary.

"Please leave us, Jodear and shut the door."

Mrs. Linnett seated herself on the bed. "Lizzie, I have been worried about you for some time and have been suspicious that your behaviour has not been what it should be," patting the bed. Lizzie came forward and sat beside her mother. "My excuse is that I've always had to be busy. There were never enough maids after the trouble at your father's business," she sighed.

"That's the trouble, Mother," said Lizzie sullenly. "You never do have time for any of us."

"But dear, that does not excuse bad behaviour," her grey eyes kindly. "I've spoken to Nanny and she's also worried about you."

"Nanny is a horrid old cat. She won't let me carry Sarah anywhere."

"Lizzie!"

"Sorry, Mother, but — "

"Other people, all of us, will have

152

a disgust of you, my dear, if you continue to kick up such a dust at every opportunity — as Jed would say," she added quickly.

"And that's another thing. When I get married, I certainly won't have any brothers or sisters. They're awful."

Mrs. Linnett controlled a quivering lip.

"Now what about the washing? I believe from what you said just now, that you are quite sure someone will do your share?"

"I'm sorry," throwing herself into her mother's arms. "I'll try and do better," then sat up indignantly, "I've much to bear."

Mrs. Linnett took the little girl on to her lap. "What is the matter, dear? Why do you behave so badly?"

Lizzie cuddled up to her mother. "Mama, please hold me tighter. You haven't done this for a very long time," she whispered. "I've been sort of at the end of the chain. Nobody bothers about me, or hears what I want to say and now baby Sarah has arrived. It's going to be worse," and burst into tears.

"Have you ever made the least effort to come and help me in whatever I've had to do?"

Lizzie shook her head.

"On this trip, we'll all have more time for each other and I expect better from you, Lizzie. Here, let me dry those tears."

All from the same source, all different, thought Mrs. Linnett and went to seek out the Captain.

She found him relaxing under an awning in front of his cabin, but rose quickly to offer her a chair, beaming hugely. "Now in what way may I be of service to you, Ma'am?"

"Would it be possible for me to have a kitten? I've seen several cats roaming about. I'd like to give it to Lizzie. She's in need of something in her life and I thought perhaps a kitten?"

"Bound to be a litter some place. Being difficult, is she?" Mrs. Linnett nodded mutely. "Speaking from vast experience, I've found that young 'uns usually grow up fairly decent human beings, Ma'am."

★ ★ ★

The children revelled in the free and easy life on board ship and soon became as brown as nutmegs, much to their mother's dismay, as she had always been secretly proud of her daughters' fair complexions, whilst Jed's language became richly larded with phrases picked up from the good-natured crew.

The day came, however, when Mr. Linnett deemed it high time to bring out the school books, much to Jed's disgust, saying that he was learning a great deal about more interesting things.

As *The Barberos* approached the tropics, the heat became oppressive and cabin doors remained opened, the family spending their free time under an awning which the Captain had had erected. It also became a favourite spot for the two officers and Captain Blyth, where they could relax after a strenuous bout of duty, while Mrs. Linnett and the girls sewed or mended and watched baby Sarah.

Joanna and Herbert argued about every subject that interested them, while Beth tried to coax Willy out of his shyness.

Both nice men, decided Mr. Linnett, looking over the tops of his spectacles, in a fatherly manner, at the group of young people before him.

Lizzie's kitten jumped up and settled on his knee. The Captain, on Lizzie's eleventh birthday, had presented her with a white and tan bundle of fur, much to her joy and spent hours with the little creature.

The family learnt a little more about the young men's background. Willy, a studious young man, was destined for the Royal Navy the following year, so carrying on his family's tradition, while

Herbert, a little older, was quite happy to stay on with the Captain.

"Mr. Bradford, please tell me about your home. Where are you from?" Joanna wanted to know.

"London and my father is Royal Navy," he replied, dabbing his face with a handkerchief. "Two sisters, twins, simpering Misses both. I was very glad to sail again.

"Thank goodness you don't simper, Miss Joanna. You are so natural, so nice. That's the first thing I noticed about you. So many young ladies' manners these days, seem to be contrived for the males' benefit. But why is your sister so sad?" with a change of subject.

"Father wouldn't give his consent to a certain proposal, but I shouldn't be discussing this."

"We'll all know a great deal about each other before we reach journey's end. Bound to, Miss Joanna," murmured Herbert, appreciating the lovely picture she made in her white muslin gown, with its multicoloured ribbons.

"Care to come for a walk around the deck?" he asked lazily.

Joanna declined just as lazily saying it was far too hot, in her friendly, tomboyish way.

Herbert was piqued. He had never met such a person as this girl, her gentle elusive charm teased him, doing nothing for his male ego. Here they were, two young people thrown together on a prolonged voyage. Surely a little dalliance would be very pleasant?

It was during one of these get togethers, that the doctor, in passing, had seen Mr. Willett place a hand on Beth's then had withdrawn it quickly. Did this mean that Mr. Willett and Beth had a liking for each other?

I'd like to punch his nose, he thought furiously, surprised at his reactions.

The Captain, amused, guessed his doctor's feelings, his bushy eyebrows working violently to suppress his chuckle and said to Beth who was sitting beside him.

"I've heard that you don't like my doctor's manners." He frowned. "I have never found him ungentlemanly, myself."

"It's just me, Captain Blyth," she said ruefully, her cheeks pink.

"Is that so?" he replied with a wealth of meaning.

Beth nodded. "We seem to strike sparks off each other."

"Lassie, we don't go through life liking everyone, you know," he said gently. "Now I must go and relieve Mr. Bradford or he'll be thinking I've fallen overboard."

The Captain left Beth in an unsettled frame of mind. The doctor's bad manners and indifference, was a hurtful experience, one she had never encountered before in her short life. Why couldn't she just ignore him, but the real reason, which she wouldn't even admit to herself, was that she would like to get to know Jonathan Barber better. They couldn't go on like this. Australia was still a distant land, not that she would ever condone his bad manners, but she found him interesting.

★ ★ ★

As the days passed, Joanna found herself thinking more and more about Jade Place, the Martins and the Stranger, daydreaming, living again that dreadful night when the workers had revolted against, what they deemed to be devilish machines, that would destroy their future. And who was the Stranger who had burst into that storeroom, black clothed and masked? Lived again her moment of panic, then the reassurance, as she caught his laughing, searching eyes, as if to engrave her face on his memory? Remembered the fluttering response of her senses when he had kissed her and the deep voice saying, "Well done, little one," and then he was gone. That sincere compliment had warmed her heart as never had the sugar-sweet nothings whispered in her ear at dances.

Those children had known him. Their loyalty had to be acknowledged and applauded.

Her rambling thoughts went on, as she shifted her position in the chair she had brought out to sit under the awning on the Quarterdeck. Freddie, what was he doing, she wondered and suddenly experienced a loneliness of the soul, which left her in a fine muddle and was relieved when Beth joined her.

"All the washing done?" she enquired.

Beth nodded. "Do you know, Jodear, that Lizzie is becoming quite civilised. She was a big help today. Only a few moans about her hands. Wonder what Mother said to her to change her like this?"

"Something pretty severe, I should think. Thank goodness. Any more encounters with the doctor?"

However, for once, Beth refused to be drawn, only shaking her head. She needed time to ponder on what had occurred earlier on in the morning.

She had met the doctor in the laundry room greeting him calmly, but with an admonishing gleam in her eyes.

He had paused and regarded her in a measuring way, which did nothing to soothe her feelings.

"Miss Beth, am I correct in thinking that you have a burning zeal to reform me?"

"No! All I ask of you is a civil greeting every time we see each other."

Suddenly, much to her surprise, he had taken her hand in his and gently kissed it. "You shouldn't have to do the washing."

She snatched away her hand.

The doctor had bowed in an exaggerated way. "I'm only heeding your strictures; minding my manners," he had added plaintively, then chuckled and strode off, his white coat flapping around his long legs.

Seeing the varying expressions on Beth's face made Joanna say, "I think you're falling in love with Jonathan Barber."

"No! I'm not."

"Oh, Bethie! So untruthful," and Joanna whisked herself into the cabin.

★ ★ ★

The time came when the lazy days aboard ship began to pall, the sea held no more appeal and the restrictive life to irritate, except for Jed who, when lessons were over, was seen no more, only appearing at meal times. The food too, left much to be desired.

When a change did come, it left the family and the ship's company appalled and decimated.

As *The Barberos* approached the tropics, the oppressive, stifling heat and damp, had an enervating effect that made the family languid and a little short of temper. Clothes sprouted mildew.

Mrs. Linnett suggested to Nanny, that perhaps certain garments could be dispensed with, under such trying conditions. The young ladies thought it prudent not to reveal that they had already discarded surplus garments.

Joanna sought out the shady nook where the rest of the family had congregated and sat down thankfully on to the deck.

"I'll never complain about a cold rain-drenched countryside ever again," she vowed. "I'll never *see* a wet English summer again," she mourned a sharp regret catching her unawares and welcomed Herbert when he dropped down beside her.

Several days later, disaster struck. The full-rigged sailing ship *The Barberos*, from the Port of London, bound for Australia via the Cape of Good Hope, other smaller ports and Port Natal struck the doldrums.

The Captain had, over the past few days, consistently reported that this could happen as the winds had dropped alarmingly. Now the sails lay furled and Lizzie, once again, likened the ship to a tree, stripped of its summer foliage.

It was an eerie experience, the ship

wallowing like a stranded whale on a deep blue sea. Mr. Linnett likened the stricken vessel, to a horrifically hot, burial casket and he was not in the habit of being so fanciful.

The sailors kept a constant day and night vigil for pirates on the alert for plunder.

The days seemed endless as they stretched into weeks. Sailors fell ill and several had died from scurvy. The doctor was stretched to his limit.

One afternoon Beth asked her father if she could offer her help with the nursing, as an alarming amount of men were now ill, the death rate high. Most days saw burials at sea, Mr. Linnett officiating, as he had taken most of the Sunday services for the Captain as he was a lay preacher.

Joanna too asked if, perhaps she could be of some use, writing letters to the deceased families.

Mr. Linnett gave his consent and approached the Captain who was visibly touched by the young ladies' offer.

Joanna would be a great help as the death notices and correspondence were mounting up, but was very reluctant that Beth should undertake some of the nursing. He had a very good idea how his doctor would react.

It was unfortunate that the Captain had not told Jonathan of Beth's offer, busy with other matters, so when Beth had taken matters into her own hands, it was she who had to face the irate man.

"What is wrong about my offer?"

"To be my nurse? My dear girl! What do you think you would be able to do?"

Beth raised an eyebrow objecting to his mode of address.

The doctor's expression had not changed and Beth thought wrathfully, that he wasn't even aware of what he had called her.

"I'm offering my help, Doctor Barber."

He exploded.

"You are offering to help nurse those

166

poor devils down there? You, a gently nurtured girl, to face that hell that is there in the hold? Over my dead body!"

Anger was in his eyes, reflecting too, his tiredness and frustrations, lines on his forehead, that she hadn't noticed before.

Beth, her fair hair a riot of curls, gazed at him steadily.

"I'll notify the Captain of your offer."

"Don't you mean ask? Anyway, the Captain has already given his permission. Subject to your consent," she added fairly. "Joanna and I have been in the habit of tending the sick amongst our workers. My father owned a manufactory in London and he cared for his people. Joanna is to help with the death notifications and correspondence. We both want to help."

His grey-green eyes snapped. "I'll remind you, Miss Linnett, that I'm the doctor of this ship and I don't give my permission."

"Very well, Sir, then I'll bid you good day, but I have nursed in some very grim places," and turned on her heel.

Jonathan, however, had caught her smile which suddenly disarmed him. He could certainly do with some help. Taking her by the arm he led her to a shady nook, turned her around and looked down into her calm face.

"Miss Beth, what would you be able to do? There is no cure for this disease. Those poor souls are just fading away. They become weaker and weaker by the day." He paused, then decided. "Come with me," taking her arm again and led her to the companionway and down to the lower deck. "You must see for yourself, before you make up your mind about this." He stopped, looking back to warn her. "It will not be a pleasant sight."

Beth nodded. "I'm no flibbertigibbet, Sir."

A welcome laugh rang out from the man beside her as they entered the vast area of the lower deck. The whole space was filled with the sick lying on rough pallets.

Beth blenched at the sight, her hand going to the doctor's arm as the stench and heat hit her. She pulled herself together. Sick were the same here as in any two-roomed cottage. They all needed help and a loving, caring word.

"Oh, these poor souls! What dreadful conditions there are down here."

"Where else do you think we could put them?" he asked bitterly.

Doctor Jonathan led Beth back up the companionway.

"I do need your help, Miss Beth, desperately and so do the patients. As the sickness takes its toll and death stalks, so there are fewer men to attend to the living's needs. If this calm lasts much longer, the Captain will be hard pushed for men to sail his vessel.

"You'll be very welcome if you come tomorrow, but I'll not blame you if you do not wish to."

Beth nodded numbly and he watched her go.

Much to his surprise, Beth presented herself the following morning. The doctor took her to a storeroom and handed her a smock and cap, showed her a room in which she could change. When she came out again, he smiled at her appearance. Her calm, hazel eyes were too large in her small face, its pure lines accentuated by the large mob-cap, her body swathed in the ankle-length gown.

"Just a little too wide." He rummaged in a drawer and brought out a sash, which he tied around her waist.

Beth lowered eyes in confusion. The doctor appeared not to notice and Beth was grateful that he had passed no mocking remark.

All he said was, "You'll do as I say, Miss Linnett." He was not finished with her, however. He turned her around and gathered up her hair.

She spun around. "What are you doing?" she asked indignantly.

"I'm going to plait your hair, if you'll allow me." He was remarkably dexterous. "I have sisters," dropping the pigtail into the back of her smock. "Tomorrow, please push it all under your cap."

Beth was surprised at the pleasure this simple operation gave her, especially when he tucked a stray curl behind her ear.

"Miss Linnett, if any sailor says a rough word to you or anything else that is out of order, I'll black his eye," grinning at her shocked expression.

"There won't be any trouble. You'll be an angel of light to those men down there. Now please come with me," and led the way down the companionway, Beth hanging back. "A gentleman takes precedence, in case you should trip."

"A soft landing, I suppose," she murmured.

There was no joking after that. The day was one she would never forget.

Beth helped where she could, the men humbly grateful for what she could do. Listened to their stories of their families, wrote letters, fed the men who were incapable of helping themselves, even closing their eyes when they died. Most of them slipped quietly away. From time to time she saw the doctor pass down the rows of pallets, the men bandying jokes with him and Beth was very conscious of their humble adoration, as their sunken eyes followed him on his inspection rounds.

At the end of that long day, the doctor led her up the companionway and out into the air which she gulped down with great breaths. Tiredness had taken over and she walked like a zombie.

The doctor shook her gently. "Miss Linnett, I have a cabin made ready for you, on the Quarter deck, where you will shed all your clothes, bathe and wash your hair. It must be carbolic soap, I'm afraid. Nanny will be there with clean clothes. She understands that scurvy is not contagious, but we'll take all precautions.

"Your shoes, you have on, wear again tomorrow and use them only when you are on duty. Nanny will see that your clothes will be laundered and a fresh gown and cap will be available each morning. Beth, are you listening to me?"

She nodded and did not even notice the use of her name and then the tears came. Sinking down, in a crumpled heap, onto a coil of thick rope, she gulped and cried like a child.

"Those poor men!" she sobbed. "What a horrible death shut away down there," starting to wipe her eyes.

The doctor quickly prevented her. "Your hands are dirty. Here, let me mop you up," wiping her face with a clean handkerchief. He crouched beside her letting her sob out her grief on his shoulder.

"Now, please stop your weeping. You managed extremely well. Today, because of your — your caring for those poor devils, some died happily. I'll not blame you if you miss tomorrow."

"No, I said I'd help. It was just a bit of a shock."

"It was darned awful!" picking her up. "Come, let me wrap my cloak around you. The evening air is chilly after the heat of the lower deck. You'll go straight to bed, Beth, doctor's orders."

She was grateful for the cloak and cuddled down in its folds as they went up to the Quarterdeck.

"Those men today, experienced a little bit of heaven in their otherwise sordid lives. I'm envious," and then he was gone.

"Oh, Nanny, it was so very awful," sobbed Beth.

"Get out of those clothes, dear and I'll bathe you just like I used to do when you were a little girl and Doctor Jonathan said you had to have a cinnamon drink after your supper which is waiting for you in your cabin."

Nanny continued in this soothing vein, Beth quite content with her ministrations. Indeed, she was a little girl again.

Before she fell asleep, behind her tired eyes was a memory of a pair of grey eyes, shot with green that could mock or smile at their owner's will.

4

BETH continued to go each day down into the hold, correctly dressed, hair plaited. As the days turned to weeks, she learnt to respect the doctor. She could do no less, thankful that her dislike had disappeared. Under the present circumstances it would have been petty. The long, tiring hours he worked and his compassion caught at her heart.

The doctor, seeing her pensiveness, raised an eyebrow. Beth, ever frank blurted out. "I still do not condone your manners, Doctor Jonathan, but you have all my respect."

"Half a loaf is better than no bread," he bowed.

That man was outrageous, like an eel, yet she found herself looking out for that tall, upright figure, needing the knowledge of his presence.

It was over the matter of Sam that she, once again, called the doctor's wrath on to her defenceless head. Beth had become very fond of the old man who knew he was dying, his one wish being to die in the open air. This had become an obsession with him. He had asked Beth if she could do anything, anything to get him up on to the top deck.

"But, Sam, how could I manage that? You know it would cause trouble. That's favouritism," but she continued to mull over the old man's need until an idea did come to her and went to see Sam again.

"Sam, the only way I can get you to the top, is if you're dead," she whispered.

The old man was bright and knew, immediately what she had in mind.

"Now, have you any trusted friends who will wrap you in your blanket and take up, topside?"

The next morning when Beth went on duty, she noticed two men carrying a shrouded figure. They both winked at her. Sam was on his way and followed the men.

She drew aside the blanket and was met with a wide toothless grin, his eyes eloquent with thanks.

"I'll go quietly and happy now, Missie."

Beth watched amazed. The hard lines of dissipation and vice slowly faded as the old sailor breathed his last. Holding his gnarled hand in her small one, his last breath was a tiny sigh of pure contentment.

Beth gently folded the old salt's arms across his chest and closed the sightless eyes.

"Sleep well in the Lord, Sam," she murmured, tears running down her cheeks.

The following morning the storm broke. The doctor was waiting for Beth.

"Now we'll have the gloves off, Miss Beth Linnett, if you please. How could you have taken Sam up top?" he asked bitingly.

"Oh, it was quite easy, surprisingly so."

"That's not what I mean and you know it. Who helped you?"

"You're a horrid man. That old sailor's one wish was to die under God's blue heaven. And how did I do it? He was included in that last batch of corpses."

"You're fortunate that we haven't had a riot on our hands."

"I cared for that old man," she said simply. "He was supremely happy when he died."

"Caring isn't enough if it creates a precedent. All these men wish to die out in the open. As I said before, it could have caused trouble."

Indignation coursed through Beth's veins as she retorted tartly. "At least one poor man had his wish granted."

The doctor glared back at her, hands raised, eyes turned upwards, then a reluctant grin lightened his anger as he said ruefully, "You'll be the death of me. Please don't do that again."

In the silence that followed, he surveyed his nurse with surprising mildness, as if her outburst, so unlike her, had cooled his own fury.

She suddenly giggled, a tiny spurt of laughter.

"That's better," approved the doctor, "although, if I'm not mistaken, that was a nervous reaction. I don't think you are the firebrand you try to make yourself to be. Now that sister of yours — "

"Jodear does stand up for herself, but perhaps I'm not very good at it yet," and found herself, much to her surprise, telling him about Bertie and her vow not to be pushed around anymore.

"It hasn't made you bitter, though. My case was similar, only I was jilted, practically at the church door. Happens to men who sail the seas. I developed a hard shell. Now do you think we could bring ourselves to see to the wants of those poor souls? Do you think you could call me Jonathan. I'd like that?"

His smile transformed his face and

Beth found the oddest weakening of her knees.

"Gemima!" breathed Beth, borrowing Joanne's favourite expression and followed the doctor.

That night, her sleepy head on her pillow, Beth reflected, with surprise, that she was happier than she had been for months. Bertie hadn't been thought of for weeks and could see in retrospect, Bertie going off most evenings to gamble, afterwards charmingly penitent, and felt a freeing of her spirit. She had been tipped into another life, another world. Everything had changed, even her feelings.

★ ★ ★

One morning Herbert visited the saloon where Joanna was busily writing. He frequently did this when he was off duty, helping her with the correspondence.

"Your watch finished?"

"Yes, thank goodness. I admire you for coming here day after day. I at least have a break and it's much cooler on the bridge. Have a break now, I've brought you some tea."

She sat back in her chair thankfully and accepted the hot beverage, longing for a glass of fresh milk.

Herbert glanced at her hot face, her fringe sticking to her forehead. "You don't have to do this, you know."

"Yes, I do. I'm being useful. I shudder when I think of the conditions under which Beth and Jonathan are working. Beth is dead tired when she comes up to bed. I haven't had a real talk with her for days and Jonathan looks as if he hasn't had a decent sleep in weeks."

Herbert nodded soberly. "It's devilishly grim down there." There was a pause then he continued, "Willy and I are most grateful to you, Joanna, for what you have undertaken. We would have had to do the lot ourselves. Doesn't bear thinking of. Care to take a stroll around the deck?" he suggested persuasively.

She readily agreed, as she normally took a break at midday.

"You're a charming person, Joanna," he said his eyes saying much more than the words implied.

"There isn't much of a choice is there?" she teased. "Only Beth and I." Her dark blue eyes, so richly lashed, laughing at him with a lazy tolerance.

Joanna got on very well with Herbert, although she often disconcerted him, when she interrupted his compliments to ask him the name of some fish that leapt out of the water.

Herbert took her arm and swung her around to face him, wondering what her reaction would be if he kissed her.

"Joanna, I — I — "

"Don't, please, Herbert, she replied swiftly. "I'm not prepared to enter into a flirtation with you, to while away the time."

"You're certainly a most disturbing person. Will you let me visit you when I'm in Australia?"

"Of course. You'll all be most welcome whenever *The Barberos* is in port. You know that."

"There are still many more weeks before we reach down under," he added hopefully.

Meanwhile, Mr. Linnett was sitting beside his wife as she fed Sarah, feeling the pangs of self-reproach, which were recurring more and more often as the days went by. He blamed himself for this terrible situation they were in, his gaze on his baby daughter.

"It's a miracle that you are still able to feed her yourself, but you, my love, are sadly thin. I must have been mad to even contemplate a trip on a sailing ship, with a four month old baby. I was too hasty."

Eliza's hand went up to stroke her husband's face. "The wind will blow again, my dear," was all she found to say.

"Dear God, when though?" He sighed and kissed her. "It's time I went to see how the children are

184

getting on with their lessons. I'm glad to say that Lizzie's lessons and manners have improved. Jed is doing well. He's the only one who is revelling in this trip."

"I'm proud of the way Beth and Joanna are helping out," said Mrs. Linnett. "And you, Joseph, for giving those poor souls spiritual help."

★ ★ ★

Captain Blyth, during this time of calm, had kept his sailors fully occupied, those that were able. Every part of the ship shone, the deck scrubbed and holystoned, the rigging checked and all sails patched.

"Captain, why do you work your men so hard and in this awful heat?" Jed wanted to know, seating himself at the Captain's feet.

"Discipline, my lad, discipline. Remember the old saying 'The devil finds work for idle hands to do?' These men are so tired by the end of the day

185

that they fall into their hammocks, with no energy to do aught else. We are all prone to fears, some even become deranged, under conditions such as these. I've even known men to riot."

"Ever thought of buying a steamship, Sir?"

The Captain was shocked.

"One of those steam kettles? Nay! Seamanship is an honourable profession, it needs skill, but driving a steam kettle? Bah!"

The Captain too, had lost a great deal of weight, his skin hanging loose about him like a pup's.

"You'd get from one port to the other much quicker and your men wouldn't die from scurvy."

"Aye, those poor devils! I've lost a lot of my crew."

"They're not devils," Jed firing up. "Some of them were my friends."

"Aye and mine," replied the Captain gruffly. "They're in a better place now, I'd be thinking. God rest their souls."

Jed agreed a little uncertainly and

went off to join the men fishing over the sides of the vessel.

"When this trip is over," he vowed, "I'll never eat another fish again."

"Be thankful, lad. 'Tis filling our bellies. Better than salted pork, any day. Never have I seen such a calm."

"Oh, look! Dolphins! I must call the others," and raced off.

Several schools had made their appearance from time to time, cavorting around the ship, much to the family's delight and were charmed by these huge, friendly mammals, believing their high, chirping noises were an effort to make contact with their human guests.

It was Jed who noticed that the sailors never harpooned these creatures and found out that there were deep superstitions among the men, that dolphins saved shipwrecked sailors taking them to shore in some magical way.

Sharks hung about in ever increasing numbers as the death rate increased.

These were harpooned and salted. Food supplies were getting low, the dry goods damp and weevily. At Mrs. Linnett's suggestion, the flour and oats were spread out on canvas sheets in the sun where the damp was lessened and the pests driven out.

Fortunately it rained often. The water barrels were scrubbed daily, upturned to dry and were always kept full.

The Captain was heard to remark that without water *The Barberos* would have become a ghost ship weeks ago.

★ ★ ★

Beth went on duty one morning to find Jonathan more depressed than usual as he reported more deaths.

"What is the use of doctors if someone can't find a way to keep fruit and vegetables fresh. This is what the men need."

"Don't blame yourself, Jonathan. You've done your best. Now with the event of the steamship, perhaps a way will be found. Anyway, a steamship cannot be becalmed."

"And what about the sailing ships?" He sighed and shook his head. "Come, I have another patient for you to meet. He's a young lad, a protégé of the Captain's and when he's older, will be a midshipman, but he's not gaining strength after a bout of fever."

Kirk was a boy of Jed's age, very frail as he lay on his bunk in a small cabin off the Captain's. His face brightened when he saw the doctor and Beth.

"I've brought you my nurse to see you," and poured him a dose of medicine.

Beth smiled at him sympathetically. "I know just how you are feeling. What you need is a diversion. When I had the influenza, I wished I could die. Just leave it to me."

Kirk was too bashful to utter a word, but there was a warmth in his brown eyes, beneath a thatch of dark, brown hair.

"May I know what you are planning?"

asked the doctor once they were outside the cabin.

"Could you ask the Captain to allow him to attend Jed and Lizzie's lessons?"

"Do you think that is the incentive to get him back on his feet? What boy likes lessons?"

"What about sending Lizzie to him?" she suggested brightly.

"Heaven help him!" hooted the doctor with derision, "but it would certainly make him fly from his bunk, just to get rid of her."

Beth grinned. "What about Jed, then?"

"That's a more sensible idea."

She was suddenly aware that the doctor was staring at her. "Have I a smut on my nose, or something?" she demanded.

He shook his head. "You have a flight of the most endearing frekles across your small, straight nose and cheeks. Don't worry," he hastened to add, "I like them. Makes you look like an urchin."

His mouth quivered at her indignation and chuckling went back to his patient. What a pity they hadn't remembered to order citron water from Mr. Holmes, the Apothecary, she thought regretfully.

★ ★ ★

Jed and Lizzie visited Kirk that same afternoon. He was horrified at their intrusion and tried to burrow further into his bunk, demanding to know from Jed, whom he already knew, why Lizzie had come.

"She insisted on coming."

"I'm the nurse," she said importantly and held out a rosy apple. "You may play with my kitten too."

"Will you pipe down, you little windbag and go away. Told you you shouldn't have come." This from Jed, but the offer of an apple won the day and Kirk ate it ravenously, sinking his teeth into its juicy crispness.

"Oh, Miss! That was good!" he said chewing and swallowing the core.

"It was mine. We all get one each day. Father brought boxes of them. You shall have mine until you get well," she promised handsomely.

Kirk was struck dumb. Never before had anyone given him anything like this and didn't know what to say. The kitten was purring on his chest, his fingers stroking the soft fur.

Jed tried to get in two words but was unsuccessful.

"Now, what would you like to do most of all? That is what Mother asks when we've been ill."

"I want to get out of this cabin."

"I don't see why not. I'll go outside while Jed helps you to dress."

This was too much for Jed, who forcibly ejected her from the cabin, much to Kirk's relief.

Kirk recovered rapidly, Lizzie keeping her promise, until the doctor gave him a clean bill of health.

The Captain gave his permission and Kirk joined the daily lessons.

"He's a bright lad and I've taught

him subjects other than the art of sailing. He'll eventually become, I hope, a midshipman. He's quite handy, helping Mac, my personal servant."

"The lad appears to be a cut above the usual rough sailor," commented Mr. Linnett.

"Yes, he is. I've asked no questions, naturally, one doesn't. I liked the look of him and he's been with me for two years now."

"He must have run away from home."

"As a lot of boys have done."

★ ★ ★

There was no letup of the dread disease as it continued to take its toll. Burial services were commonplace and the sharks continued to haunt the waters.

Mr. Linnett was called in most nights to minister to the dying, when the spirit was at its lowest, the lanterns casting eerie shadows around the huge deck, the men's faces weird as they lay on their grass pallets, others in hammocks. His tall prophetic figure with its white hair and beard and friendly smile quickly lessened the shouting and muttering. On occasions he would break into a well-known hymn, his rich baritone reaching every corner of this hellhole, the tune taken up by dozens of hesitant voices, as if it had been many years since any hymn had passed the lips of these hardened sailors.

As Beth went off one late afternoon, Doctor Jonathan told her she could take a day off.

"You're looking fagged to death, Beth," and she was only too glad to comply.

If anyone had told him that it would be Beth, resembling thistledown, would be the one who had the quiet strength of mind and spirit to help him with all these tragic patients of his, he would have laughed. His choice would have been Joanna, sturdy, independent.

He watched Beth go up the companionway, a great peace in his heart, which he hadn't experienced since Marla had given him his congé, for Keith who had been his best friend.

* * *

After her day's rest, Beth waited for the doctor to come up from the deck below. She had slept most of the day, in spite of the heat and was much refreshed.

"I've missed you today," were his first words and she noticed bottomless tiredness clouding his eyes and her concern reached out to him.

"Please go off now and sleep. I'm feeling much better, thank you. You need a night off," but he shook his head. "Please, what will happen to all of us — the men, if you fall ill? I'll spend the night here and Mac will be on duty as well."

The doctor straightened up angrily, "What in the name of of — flying fishes — . You take too much on yourself. You that a puff of wind could — " then slumped again. "Yes, I'm tired," and Beth knew what that cost him. "I'm grateful, Beth," a travesty of a smile curving his mouth.

"You'll feel much better tomorrow," she said bracingly.

"It would appear that we've changed places?"

"I wouldn't dare to presume!"

His laugh was hollow. "What I want to know is, how you managed to wind the Captain's very correct gentleman's gentleman, around that little finger of yours?"

Beth's smile was impish. "Gentle methods, I've found, work wonders, doctor," with a wealth of innuendo.

He acknowledged the hit and went off to his cabin gratefully.

After a refreshing night's sleep the doctor came on duty early to find Beth at the rail, her weary legs heavy, her head splitting. It had been a strange night, the men in a strange mood, almost expectant, some of the old sailors prophesying that a wind was on its way.

A fiery dawn sky was now holding her attention. Scarlet and blue rays fanned up from the eastern horizon, that would remain in her memory forever. Leaning tiredly on the rail she murmured, "'Red sunset at night, a shepherd's delight, red in the morning, a shepherd's warning.'"

It was a prayer.

"Oh," she cried out and turned around in fright. "Oh, it's you. You startled me."

"You were so engrossed with the sunrise that I did not wish to disturb you."

Still a tired man, thought Beth and her heart went out to him and for all those men down there in the hold who wouldn't see another sunset or sunrise.

"Are you all right, Beth?" he asked anxiously. "You look dreadful. Let me feel your face," his long sensitive fingers lingering on her forehead.

"No, only tired. Do you think that little rhyme about red sunsets and red sunrises will really be true for us?"

He replied soberly, "I hope and pray that it will be so. I've also been watching and wondering."

He went on. "Beth, you are a very unusual and exceptional person. I can't think of a single girl of my acquaintance, or even in my family, who could or would have undertaken what you have done during these weeks. Don't you think you could call me Jonathan, without the 'doctor'? We've been through so much."

"Jonathan," she said obediently and nodded.

He took her arm and guided her to where Nanny was waiting. "You're tired out and no wonder," and dropped a light kiss on her cheek. "Thank you Beth, for changing a very cynical man into a different being. You've restored my faith in womanhood."

★ ★ ★

Very early the following morning, a gale blew up. Dense billowing clouds flew over the moon, the dawn incandescent pink and white.

The Barberos was on her way again at last, its hull creaking as if in protest at its long sleep being disturbed. The sails again were unfurled, billowy with the fierce wind.

The family hurriedly dressed after Jed had burst in. "We're moving, we're moving," he had yelled then disappeared again to become part of the wildly jubilant crew and officers.

The whole family were soon at the rails of the quarterdeck.

"Praise God from whom all blessings flow," shouted Mr. Linnett and others took up the chant of praise.

Later Joseph, holding his wife close, murmured, "I'll never forget this sunrise. 'From the dawn of the morning, the day is brought forth.'"

"From the Psalms, of course," replied Eliza softly.

Everyone was rejoicing madly, the

Captain a new being as he roared out his orders to the sailors who scurried about frantically. At midday, he ordered all men on deck and a Thanksgiving Service was held. Every head was lifted in grateful praise as the men began to softly sing Handel's Hallelujah chorus, the beautiful words and music ringing to the Heavens in ever increasing volume.

It was a truly wonderful, exhilarating sight to see the snapping sails fat with wind and feel the ship once more dancing through the high waves.

The brisk wind whipped the family's clothes around their thin bodies as they hung on to the rail, feeling very much a part of this vast, primeval force, but although *The Barberos* was under way again, their troubles were by no means over. It would still be weeks before the Cape of Good Hope was sighted.

The Barberos had been becalmed for two and a half months.

5

LIFE on board ship settled down again to a humdrum existence, the family, with the exception of Jed, longing for the sight of the Cape of Good Hope and its solid feel under their feet. The younger children had longer school hours which did much to relieve Lizzie's boredom, while Mrs. Linnett, Beth and Joanna found an hour or so to either sew or mend. Even the doctor felt free, now that the scurvy cases had lessened, to take time off to relax, sitting with the ladies enjoying watching their activities, which he said was soothing in the extreme and even, sometimes to fall asleep, Beth watching him tenderly, stretched out on the deck.

Out of her great admiration for Jonathan and his ceaseless care of his patients, love had been born, a love that was true and deep. She had acknowledged this to Joanna as they made ready for bed one evening.

"Oh, Jodear, his unstinting attention for those poor souls down in that stinking hold, I'll always remember. Yes, I love Doctor Jonathan. This is no romantic infatuation such as I had for Bertie. We've gone through so much together."

Joanna was ecstatic, hugging her sister and dancing around the cabin with her. "Oh, Bethie love! I'm so happy for you. I'm sure Jonathan will propose to you soon."

"Perhaps he doesn't love me," she said sadly remembering all his cynicism.

Once again, as had happened on the first night on *The Barberos*, as Beth lay on her bed, she heard someone playing a flute, a haunting, evocative melody, that pulled at her heart strings, her longing and love overspilling, causing the tears to flow.

Would she ever be able to sweep

away the expression of coldness from his eyes?

The family were again invited to dine with the Captain and afterwards to attend a dance which would be held on the deck, Herbert having organised chairs and had had a space cleared.

The three girls were very excited at the chance to wear their pretty dresses, after the months of calm when no entertainment had been held.

Beth had taken Lizzie in hand and was combing her brown, curly hair into a topknot, finishing it off with a rosette of net to match her pink muslin dress.

The little girl was ecstatic. "Do you think Kirk will be there, at the dance, I mean? And will Mother allow me to dance?"

"Lizzie, you are a bit young, you know," Joanna teased and then relented. "We have become like one big family here, so perhaps Mama will allow you, but," she added hastily, "that is only my opinion. Thank goodness, Beth, no-one will know that our gowns are years old. I used to suffer agonies over that."

Even so, both the girls made an attractive picture as they left the cabin to meet their escort. Jonathan had promised to carry out this pleasant duty.

Beth, in a rose-pink gown with darker pink ribbons, hoped that he would pass some remark, after seeing her for weeks enveloped in smock and mob-cap. Surely he would do so, but except for a smile and a bow he made no comment as he shepherded all the girls to the Captain's suite.

"What a change from your white coat, doctor," Beth said pointedly.

Jonathan chuckled. "You all made a delightful picture. I'm indeed honoured to escort such a bevy of beauties."

They all smiled and Beth said, "Thank you. Your manners *have* improved!" but the words were gentle.

A beaming Captain welcomed the family and ceremoniously handed them over to Mac who seated them. An extra rum ration had been issued to the sailors, the Captain having also partaken somewhat liberally, with the result he was very merry, although usually, was the most abstemious of men.

All the officers were splendidly dressed, in well-cut coats and trousers, snowy white shirts, their hair newly barbered. Their appreciative glances at Beth and Joanna forecast a very pleasant evening.

At the end of the meal, the Captain led them to where several sailors, with flutes and concertinas broke into a foot tapping Strauss' waltz.

The Captain bowed and led Mrs. Linnett on to the floor, the doctor with Beth and Herbert and Joanna followed suit. Much to Lizzie's gratification, Willy asked her to dance.

They raced up the deck when it lifted and back again as it sank amid much merriment.

Much later there was a small

ceremony. The Captain rose ponderously and not too steadily, to his feet.

"Ladies and gentlemen, I have the greatest pleasure in asking Miss Beth, Miss Jodear, ahem, Miss Joanna, I like Jodear best," that person blushing to the roots of her tawny brown hair, much to Herbert's admiration. The Captain continued, "Miss Elizabeth to step forward too. These dear girls — these dear girls — " Words failed him. "Jonathan — "

"For the sterling work they have performed during our time of trial," supplied the doctor promptly, with a special smile for Beth, tinging her cheeks with flags of colour.

"Thank you," said the Captain. "Miss Jodear," this time he did not apologise, "for her hard work in writing out the official notifications of the sailors who died. God rest their souls. So many, so many," he mourned, dabbing his eyes with his handkerchief. "Miss Beth for her — " his voice cracking, "for her unstinting love and patience for all those sick and dying souls, under — under dreadful conditions. Miss Elizabeth for giving up her apple to Seaman Kirk. Bless you all, I'm proud of you."

There was loud clapping.

The Captain then presented each with a small draw-string pouch, which had a pleasant jingle to them.

Loud clapping broke out again and everyone began to talk at once, until the Captain held up his hand for silence. "Of course, let's not forget Mr. Linnett's contribution. I'm most grateful, Sir," with a bow as low as his huge girth would permit.

Everyone held their breath as they wondered if the old seadog would lose his balance.

"Ladies and gentlemen, I've not yet finished. I'd like Jed to come forward," and beamed at the boy who had a special place in his heart. "This lad has been outstanding in the performance of his duties. The ship has never been so free of rats," and handed him a similar pouch.

Beth and Joanna had each received ten golden sovereigns, Lizzie and Jed two. This was a small fortune to them and for a second were dumbfounded, then crowded around the Captain, who was much gratified when the girls kissed and hugged him, Lizzie going so far as to ask him if he would be their grandfather as they hadn't one. The old man was visibly touched and blew his nose loudly.

"I'll certainly keep in touch with you all," he promised.

Later in the evening he said to Jonathan, with a crafty look, "Well, lad, my experiment has gone very well, don't you think and what have you to say about it now?" However the doctor was not to be drawn. The Captain chuckled as he watched the doctor sweep Beth into another waltz. That little girl, if he was not mistaken, had crept under his doctor's impervious skin.

It was very late by the time the party broke up. The girls, decorously, said 'goodnight' to their parents and then Joanna waltzed Beth into their cabin, whirling her around until she begged for mercy.

"Jodear, what on earth!"

"It suddenly hit me this evening, that I love Freddie. Would you believe it? It's too late! What am I going to do?" but with this acknowledgment a peace flowed through her. A balm as beneficial as the wind snapping the sails. The stranger who had taken up much of her thoughts of late, was forgotten, Freddie's shy salute taking its place. He had been such a dear, familiar figure; too close to see properly?

Regret filled her, a regret that left a bitter taste in her mouth. "'The error of the moment becomes the sorrow of a lifetime.'"

"One of Father's Chinese proverbs. Oh, Jodear, what are you going to do now? I'm reminded of Miss

Pilkins reading to us in her thrilling, overemphasized voice from Richard II. 'Oh call back yesterday bid time return' or something like that?"

"Why didn't I wake up sooner, before we left. How will he know of my changed feelings? I've been so blind."

"Perhaps you'll meet someone else," Beth said diffidently.

"In Australia? I won't."

"Jodear, if Freddie is meant for you, I believe something will happen."

"Were you of that opinion when Father refused to sanction a marriage between you and Bertie?"

Beth shook her head. "I've met Jonathan."

* * *

The days slipped by uneasily into each other. Beth was pleased to note that Jonathan was thawing and as he did so his grey-green eyes lost their bleakness. He, himself felt more relaxed as he watched Beth's progress between the pallets, a smile and a touch for each patient. It was pathetically sad to watch these men's eyes follow her adoringly. She was indeed an angel of light in this dingy hell-hole. Fortunately the scurvy cases were lessening and the day came when surgery, once again, was held twice daily. Beth worked here during the morning, mostly to keep up the records. Too many cards had written 'Deceased' across them.

Joanna, during this time, learnt what loneliness of the spirit meant, grateful that she could still busy herself with the official forms. The deceased's personal belongings also had to be packed to be sent to the next of kin. In this matter, it was the duty of Herbert and Willy to perform this task.

Lizzie, the thorny one of the family, forgot her previous feelings of inadequacy, the child at the end of the chain, Sarah now taking that position, which to her was a source of comfort.

Mr. Linnett was again concerned about his wife. The conditions under which they lived, the poor food, the heat, must have taken its toll. They were sitting enjoying the lovely sunset one evening, his arm around her.

"My dear, you are even thinner than when I last spoke of this."

Eliza chuckled. "Jonathan has persuaded us to leave off much of our clothing. It takes me far less time now to dress and the mount of washing has certainly declined. Perhaps that is why I look thinner?"

"But are you in good health, my dear?"

"Joseph, there is absolutely nothing to worry about. I always do fine down when suckling a babe, you should know that, but what I am worried about is Joanna and Herbert."

He was startled. "But — but — "

Her troubled thoughts bubbled out. "I believe he spends much time with

212

her in the Captain's saloon."

"But, my dear, helping Joanna is Herbert's duty too and Willy's. I would have thought it makes a welcome break for Jodear. I certainly would not relish what she has to do. Official, uniform, naval notifications, which are without an ounce of sympathy."

"Oh, why didn't she fall in love with Freddie before we left?" thumping her fist into her other hand in frustration. "Too late now. He wouldn't be able to come out. Paul should come home and take up his responsibilities. A bad situation."

"I don't quite agree," murmured her odiously calm husband. "I've been noticing that Jodear has been watching Beth and the doctor and feeling a little envious. Now those two make an excellent couple. I would give my consent to that marriage, any day."

But Mrs. Linnett was not satisfied, wondering if this unnatural, transient life would induce artificial feelings that would not endure. She did not want

Beth to be hurt again, but she had lost that haunted look.

Her mind went back to the matter of Joanna and Herbert. He was a most presentable man, but — it was as if the whole situation was slipping from her grasp and said so.

"Now, now, Eliza, my dear," soothed Joseph. "Jodear is a sensible person and this abnormal existence will end. I'm at the moment, still enjoying time that I never had previously, although the food could be better, of course. My dear, please forgive me for bringing you all on this wild goose chase. If anything happens to Sarah, I'll never forgive myself."

Eliza sat up suddenly. "Joseph, I must speak what is on my mind. All these years I have deferred to you, but I'm not prepared to go all that way to Australia." She put up a hand, "No, let me finish. I've spoken to the Captain who has told me that Natal is a British colony. We'll disembark there. I'm also afraid that if my milk

214

fails, Sarah will die. I'm not willing to take that chance."

"My dear, of course we'll consider this, but we do have family over there — "

"No, Joseph, we'll settle in Natal and that's my final word."

Jonathan too had uncertain thoughts. Over the weeks, his admiration for Beth had turned into a deep and abiding love for her, but was it fair to tell her of this love? Propinquity could play the very devil and they had been thrown together into a situation that was far from normal. People did cling together in stressful circumstances.

When the rest of the family were told the news, they were all relieved and the Captain too, was in agreement.

The following afternoon, after surgery, Beth washed her hair and went out on to the deck to dry it. Meanwhile Jonathan suddenly realised that when the family disembarked at Durban, this ship would become a desert for him without Beth. Had propinquity played too great a part? Not where he was concerned and went to find her.

She noticed him coming her way and shrank back into the shade of the superstructure. Afraid that her love would show?

But Jonathan had seen her, getting down on his haunches he took the towel from her and began to rub her hair, her forehead nearly touching his chest.

"Please don't worry," mumbled Beth, thankful that her hair hid her face, but she was startled when he drew her close into his arms.

"You do know, don't you, that this is where you belong, girl dear? You are part of me, Bethie," he murmured into her fragrant hair. "Will you marry me?"

Her nod was decisive. "Oh yes, please," she breathed.

He gently parted her hair and saw her answer in her eyes and glowing face. He bent his head and his first kiss was as gentle as a butterfly's wing.

Beth felt a deep sigh go through him

and saw the tenderness in his glance.

"Here, let me open my jacket. All these buttons can't be comfortable," and drew her back into his arms and thoroughly kissed her.

Beth gladly surrendered to his kiss as his arms tightened around her, as if he would never let her go.

"I love you, Bethie. You warm my spirit. There is that dear quality in you, my love." When they came to their senses again, Jonathan said, "Where ever your family settle, I'll open a practice there."

"And I'll be your nurse, may I?" her voice eager.

"I'd appreciate that, but only until the children arrive," he teased, enjoying the lovely colour diffusing her cheeks, which she tried to hide in his shoulder. "And at the end of the day to love and be loved."

"But why were you so rude to me?"

"I was horrified when I saw you and realised we had passengers aboard."

"Because of Marla?"

217

"Yes, I was very bitter against all women, but I did notice how sad and listless you were that day and wondered if you had left a very dear person behind."

Beth shook her head. "It wasn't anything like the love I have for you, Jonathan dear."

He took up the comb and began to untangle the skeins of silky hair. "When I worked with you, day in and day out, nursing those sick sailors, I had nothing but love and respect for you. And you were no longer sad or listless. I also noticed, professionally, of course, that as you became more and more incensed by my behaviour, so you became alive again. You were determined to reform me, weren't you?" his grey-green eyes dancing mischief at her, his lips twitching out of control.

Beth's mouth dropped, her outraged expression causing Jonathan to rise to his feet, pluck Beth to hers and kiss her hard.

"Do you mean to say all those bad

manners were contrived? You — you are outrageous," she spluttered.

"Some of them." He suddenly disarmed her by that twinkle in his eyes. "Forgive me? I'll have you know, that I was only working in my professional capacity, as I said before," he replied mendaciously, then sobered. "I knew at the Captain's first dinner party, that you were the only girl for me. Now I must go and see your father. I'll be back. Please stay here," and gave her a final hug.

★ ★ ★

Beth sat quite still, savouring this enchanted happiness within her.

Jonathan found Mr. Linnett deep in some book and dropped down into a chair next to him, surprisingly a little nervous.

"Having some well earned time off?"

"Yes, Sir, but I've come to ask if I might marry Beth. Without her my life will be barren and incomplete."

Mr. Linnett chuckled, shook Jonathan's hand and said warmly, "Welcome into the family, lad. Mrs. Linnett and I couldn't wish for a nicer person for our Beth. You have our blessings, but why did you take so long?"

"Thank you, Sir," he replied with a heartfelt sigh. "I'm very happy to be part of your family and wherever you settle, as I have just told Beth, there I'll open a practice."

"Splendid! You two are blessed, Jonathan, for you know each other far better than any other couple contemplating matrimony."

"Yes, we are blessed," he agreed and rose to his feet. "I'll go and fetch Beth, Sir. We both want your blessing." He was about to go, then paused. "I'd like to marry Beth as soon as we arrive in Durban."

Mr. Linnett was startled. "So soon?"

"Just a simple ceremony, Sir. I feel as if I've lived a lifetime since we left Britain."

The Captain and the crew were

overjoyed at the news, the doctor being well liked.

"Thought you and Beth were smelling of April and May, lad. My sincerest congratulations," said the Captain.

Joanna, for a moment, knew a pang of envy. Would she ever see Freddie again, then stifled the envy. "Oh Bethie," and hugged her sister. "I'm so very pleased for you both. What a heavenly brother Jonathan will make."

She had watched this dearest of sisters slowly fall in love with the doctor and rejoiced in her joy, but it made her longing that more poignant. Suddenly, she could bear no more of this awful feeling that was tearing her apart and sought refuge in a space between two lockers, like some small animal in distress and sank on to the deck, wracking sobs tearing her body. Now she knew the love that the Brontes had written about.

Mr. Linnett, on his way to the cabin, heard the sobbing and found her in a crumpled heap, the tears wet on her face. Seeing his daughter in such distress alarmed him. Never had he known Jodear to give way to tears. He sat down, raising her into his arms.

"Oh, Papa," she sobbed into his shoulder. "I'm so glad it was you who found me."

"Jodear, what on earth — what has happened to distress you so?"

How to explain that Freddie was so much part of her now, as he would be if he were physically present? Her father's voice, though, was so gentle and affectionate, that the words came tumbling out.

"Oh, Father, I love Freddie and he's a million miles away. Why was I so blind? Why didn't I realise he loves me? He tried to tell me as he said goodbye. Too late now."

"Jodear, if he had told you of his love, what would your answer have been? The truth, please."

"I — I suppose," she gulped, "I suppose I would have gaped at him and laughed. He was only another brother," with a fresh spurt of tears.

"Now come, my dear and let me mop you up," bringing out a comfortable sized handkerchief.

"Men's ones are so much more of use than ladies' ones," she hiccoughed and blew her straight little nose fiercely.

"That's better. You looked like a drowned kitten. Now, now, don't start again. Jodear, have you forgotten that there will be letters waiting for us in Cape Town from the Martin family and also we'll be able to post ours to them?"

Joanna straightened up. "But that won't tell Freddie I love him."

"No, but you can tell him how much you miss him."

Mr. Linnett did not tell her that he had every intention of writing to Freddie to tell him of his daughter's change of heart. After all, he had promised the lad.

"I feel better already, Father. Thank you."

"Trouble shared trouble halved. A

little trite perhaps, but sound common sense none the less."

The mischievous look was back in her eyes. "I'd give much to see the letter," with a watery grin.

"That you shall not, Miss."

★ ★ ★

As the journey proceeded, Mr. Linnett marvelled at the men's and his family's ability to survive in the face of such crushing odds. A new spirit had taken over: a spirit to live, but all things have an ending. *The Barberos* at last had reached the Cape of Good Hope. The cables raced out, the smell of scorching from the ropes against the rims of the hawser holes; a welcome occurrence.

A weak cheer rang out from the half-starved crew and passengers as they fell on their knees with heads bowed under the hot African sun. Hearts were full and many were the faces with unashamed tears of joy running down them.

There, towering above them, was the famed Table Mountain bedecked with its snowy cloud covering. To the right were twelve small peaks named the Twelve Apostles and to the left, Devil's Peak.

This was indeed, the Cape of Good Hope.

★ ★ ★

Advanced as the afternoon was, the Captain sent a boat to collect the mail and within a short space of time, bags were hauled up on deck, everyone waiting eagerly for the sorting to be completed.

Joanna, seated in her favourite nook, opened Freddie's letter with fingers that shook, but it only contained family news and a detailed account of all the alterations and repairs being done to Jade Place, which were going along with all speed. It was just a normal, friendly letter, but which left her in a disappointed, depressed state of

225

mind. Was Freddie thinking of getting married, otherwise why the haste to set Jade Place to rights?

The following morning, Jonathan and Beth left the ship early as they wanted to buy the ring. They would return and later in the day join the family on a tour of the town and countryside.

"A beautiful, sparkling morning," said Beth happily as they made their way down the gangway, her hand warmly held in Jonathan's. "And you, dearest, are very distinguished in that snuff-brown coat. Ah!"

They both stood quite still as they stepped from the gangway, savouring the firm ground undcr their feet.

At that moment a carriage drew up and out stepped a beautiful woman. She was tall, dark red hair peeping out from under an extremely fetching villager hat, with ribbons that matched her spring-green gown.

Beth felt Jonathan stiffen as he tucked her hand more firmly under his arm. In a colourless voice he said, "Marla!

What a surprise!"

Eyes the colour of brown pansies, widened in response to this cool greeting, before throwing herself at Jonathan, who neatly side stepped.

"Oh, Jonathan! I'm so glad to see you! I've waited weeks and weeks. I've come to apologize for my shockingly bad behaviour but I've paid for it. Reggie was a dreadful husband."

"You are speaking of my best friend, Marla. A better man never walked this earth," his words icy.

"I've divorced him." She shuddered theatrically. "He refused to take me to any more parties or balls and what was worse, he wanted a son," she ended up indignantly.

"A very reasonable wish, surely?"

"Oh, Jonathan, you've been so much in my thoughts. I just had to see you."

"What brought you to Cape Town and where's Reggie?"

"He's gone back to England. We came out here several years ago. I'm free now, Jonathan," she exalted.

Never once did her eyes turn to Beth, nor did he think to introduce her.

"I heard from the Port authorities that *The Barberos* was long overdue. I've been in agony, thinking you were lost at sea. I've come to ask you if we could start afresh," her brown eyes appealing. "You could set up a practice here easily. This is an extremely busy port," adding eagerly, "the social life you'll love. Do you remember all the parties we used to attend? I'm a very experienced woman now."

"I'm sure you are," he replied dryly. He raised his hat. "Now we must really take our leave of you. We have some pressing business to attend to."

"Couldn't introduce you, Bethie. Didn't want to," he added gruffly, as they walked along the wharf. "You were perfect, my love. Not even a quiver of your hand," and placed his over hers. "Thank you."

"She is very beautiful."

But Jonathan could not agree, his reply scathing. "Marla never had on all that paint on her face when I knew her."

They took a hack, neither of them noticing the angry woman flounce into the carriage that had brought her, giving the driver some terse directions to a certain, well-known Tavern.

"I realised on this voyage," continued Jonathan, his arm around Beth, "that the person one falls in love with, in the early twenties, is not necessarily the same type as the one you would choose in later life. I was besotted. What a reprieve!"

He turned Beth to face him, taking both her hands in his, holding them to his chest, his eyes tender as he searched her face, then raised one hand to kiss each fingertip. "Your shyness, when you are not berating me, is a never ending delight to me, my love."

"Oh, Jonathan," breathed Beth, "I never realised that there could be so much happiness in this world."

"It's a man's love I offer to you. All of it, you know that, don't you?"

She nodded, her face radiant. "And you have mine, dearest," and shyly surrendered to his kiss, his arms tightening around her as if he would never let her go.

As they made their way back up the gangway, Jonathan said, "We'll take a trip back to England one day, to visit my parents. I'd like them to get to know and love you, too."

"On *The Barberos*?"

"I think not. We'll go by steam."

The family greatly admired the beautiful diamond engagement ring and necklace, fashioned into a shower of flowers, sapphires set in silver leaves that Jonathan had given Beth. There were hugs all around.

"Bethie, I'm so pleased you've found real love at last. Jonathan is such a dear."

"I only wish that — that you — "

"That I'd woken up before we left England?" replied Joanna wryly.

That afternoon the long expected luncheon, that the Captain had promised the family weeks ago, was held in one of the harbour's taverns and was much appreciated. Needless to say, nobody chose fish and everyone relished the fresh fruit and vegetables set before them.

After the meal the Captain excused himself as he had a great deal to do. He, however, allowed Herbert, Willy and Kirk to accompany the family on a sight-seeing expedition of Cape Town and its surrounds. Jonathan also excused himself as he had a lot of paper work still to do for the harbour authorities.

Joanna, on seeing Herbert in his off duty attire, had stared at him in frank admiration. She had never seen him in anything other than his officer's uniform and evening dress of sober black, but here he was elegantly turned out in a well-fitting coat of pale gray, darker trousers and shining boots. She wondered who had laundered his frilly, white shirt.

"You are right on the mark, Herbert,"

she had said with an admiring glance. "For a moment I didn't recognise you." He wasn't exactly handsome, she thought, but his frank open manner was pleasing.

He had watched her quizzically. "You're not so bad yourself, Joanna. I like that russet gown. I'm going to miss you sorely. I had hoped for your company until we reached Australia. Now you are all disembarking at Durban. Devilish!"

That whole afternoon proved to be a great success. They all loved the funny little shops and the strange languages that were spoken in the streets, not to mention the queer dress some people wore. It was Willy who informed them that the immigrants here in the Cape were Dutch, English and Malay, while those in Natal were mostly British

They walked a little way up Table Mountain, enjoying the wide open country and gazed down at the sea and glittering sands of the bays, filled, or so it seemed, with fishing smacks and there, far down lay *The Barberos*.

During their short stay in the Cape, the family also drove out to see the vineyards that grew so profusely on the mountain slopes and also how wine was made and stored. The old Dutch gabled houses were beautiful, with their white walls and thrown-back oak shutters. The gardens were a riot of colour.

Mrs. Linnett was loath to leave. She had not realised how flower-starved she had become.

"'The fairest Cape of all'" she murmured and knew that Sir Francis Drake had not exaggerated.

They lunched at an old Inn and eagerly crowded around a book where Captain Cook, in 1775, had written his name.

Meanwhile, the revictualling of the ship went on apace, the Captain assuring them that meals would be far more palatable.

Letters had been posted on the day they had arrived as a steamship had been sailing that evening. In Mr. Linnett's letter to Freddie was an important message. Also a forwarding address. Poste Restante Durban.

★ ★ ★

The day arrived when the family had to say farewell to this lovely Cape and continue on with their journey. The weather bid fair, so the Captain said, and it should prove that it would be a pleasant journey to Durban.

One evening Jed sought out the Captain and found him enjoying a pipe out on the deck and sat down at his feet.

"When do we reach East London?" he wanted to know and was told that it would be, probably, the following morning. "There is a lot of cargo to unload."

"Is it, at all, like Cape Town?"

The Captain shook his head, biting his pipe between stained teeth. "There is no dock there. Surf boats come out alongside and we off-load into them."

"May we go ashore?"

"Nay, lad, no time for that," glancing at the skyline. "If it does decide to blow up, the boats are incapable of coming out. That's a botheration for the unfortunate traders and the people who will have to wait for their goods until I make the return journey, but I don't foresee any trouble this time," with another look at the sky.

"Are there any other pitfalls we're likely to come across, do you think?"

"I pray not. Perhaps nature will be kind. We've had a grim time of it to date. But what's troubling you, lad?"

"There's talk amongst the sailors of a huge black hole, somewhere between here and Port Natal, that draws in ships, never to be heard of again." Jed's eyes, unusual for him, were anxious.

"Aye, that is true, but the weather forecast is good. I pray that it stays that way, but keep this information under your hat, lad. I'll not have my passengers, bless 'em, frightened out of their wits."

It was just as the Captain had foretold. A colourful scene met their eyes the following morning. Barges hugged the ship's side, the sea calm, while Africans clambered up the vessel with the aid of ropes, chanting their peculiar songs. Bales were thrown out into these flat-bottomed boats, with no account taken as to their contents.

The hatches were again closed, the workers swarmed back down and the anchor lifted.

It was beautiful scenery along the coast, swathes of sugar-cane, broken every now and again, by African *kraals*. This was the Pondoland coast, the Captain allowing the children to view the scene through his telescope. Days later he told them to keep a look out for Durban Point.

Jed, the enquiring one asked, "Why do some people call Durban, Port Natal?"

"Most folk in England do, but it was

renamed after Sir Benjamin D'Urban, a former Governor of the Cape Colony, several years back now."

Durban Point was reached at last and a gun boomed out, to notify the inhabitants that a British ship was coming in.

"It's been a long wait for this batch of mail and goods," said the Captain. "It's been a voyage that I wouldn't care to go through again and I give thanks for our safe arrival here and to thank the whole Linnett family for their fortitude under great stress." He glanced down at Gyp. "Don't know how that animal survived with a boatload of hungry sailors and all," his voice gruff.

Jed hugged his pet to him. "I enjoyed myself immensely and wish we were going on to Australia."

The Captain turned to Mrs. Linnett who was sitting next to him and said, "I believe this young firebrand of yours, Ma'am, and he would make an excellent sailor."

She smiled. "You've been kind to us, Sir, but I for one, will not be averse to land tomorrow. Permanently! Oh, for a firm space for our feet to rest on."

"I'll take you to a respectable tavern and introduce you to friends of mine who run it most successfully."

"Perhaps you could recommend a removal firm and we'll also have to find a house quickly."

"Mr. and Mrs. Andrews, who own the Tavern by the Sea, will surely be able to help you."

The Barberos arrived in the roadstead, the anchor cables rumbled through the hawser-holes, just as the sun was setting in a ball of fire, long streamers of gold and red thrown across the deep blue of the approaching night. Darkness came early to this part of the world.

The following morning the family were up betimes and went on deck. The question then arose on how they were to get ashore. This was voiced by Jed.

"You have a choice, lad, of either using the rope ladder into the waiting boat, or in the barrel," replied the Captain.

A boat was quickly lowered and two sailors scrambled down.

The young ladies did not relish either mode of disembarkation and said so in no uncertain terms.

Jed hooted in derision. "You wouldn't like the ignominy of the barrel, would you? I'll go first," and nimbly clambered down, to be helped into the boat, which was rocking alarmingly, by Jonathan, who had gone down first.

Joanna, who now knew that Jonathan would catch her, had no problem.

"Come on, Bethie," Jonathan called up, with an exhilarating sense of joy at the sight of his little love, dithering at the rail.

Beth had watched in dismay Joanna's descent, doubting whether she could venture on to that ladder with any semblance of dignity.

With heartening shouts from below

she eventually consented and wrapping her skirts tightly around her legs, stepped on to the ladder. Jonathan was quick to pluck her off and stood her on her feet, Beth indignantly breathless.

"Now I know what a sack of meal feels like."

The rest of the family elected to go over the side decorously. As they reached the shore, all looked back at *The Barberos* as she lay tranquilly on the gently moving tide. There was good and bad to remember.

Calling up two landaus the Captain handed in his passengers and gave directions to the two coachmen. The distance was short and they soon stopped in front of a two-storied building, ivy clinging to its red walls.

The Captain ushered them into the reception lounge and introduced the family to Mrs. Andrews, a large comfortable body with a beaming face, under silvery-grey hair.

"Come in, my dears and Captain Blyth, I'm happy to welcome you again.

We heard that *The Barberos* had been becalmed."

"Can you accommodate all of us?"

"Yes, of course. We're not full. What a dreadful journey you must all have had. And that poor wee mite!" with a smile for Sarah and Nanny. "Don't know how you all survived and that's a fact, but there, I'm talking too much."

The good lady shepherded the family upstairs and showed them their respective rooms which were clean and homely. "Luncheon will be served at midday. Now I will send you up some tea."

Mrs. Linnett sat down, took off her bonnet and heaved a sigh of relief. "It's so good to have solid earth under our feet again, Joseph, and a bed that does not sway continuously."

Her husband agreed, but said with some concern. "Will you be happy? We have no kith or kin here, although I have been very impressed with the little we've seen of the town."

"We're all together, my dear, and that's all that really matters. I could not have gone any further, Joseph," and suggested that he meet Mr. Andrews to ask about the property market. "The sooner we find a house, the better it will be and I think a material printing business should do very well here. Don't you agree?"

Joseph nodded his head and thought, with gratitude, of the machine they had brought with them. It had not been smashed on that fateful night when his workers had run amok, due to the fact that it hadn't been unpacked at that time and had been safe in his storeroom. His spirits soared and went off to find Mr. Andrews. He would choose a house with a large shed in the back garden and make a new start.

★ ★ ★

The Barberos was not long in port and it was sad for the whole family parting with Captain Blyth and the officers. Promises were made that they would all meet again on the return journey.

Kirk was not forgotten as the family had come to like him too.

Herbert managed to see Joanna alone for a few minutes, taking her hand in his and before she realised his intentions, placed a kiss on its palm, then closing her fingers. "Goodbye, Jodear. God keep you. We've been through so much. I've learnt to love you dearly. No one will ever take away my memories of a very lovely person. If it hadn't been for the Linnett family on board I'm sure we'd have become brutalized," and with that, Herbert was gone.

Joanna stood quite still, close to tears.

The Captain sad at having to lose his doctor, was genuinely pleased at the engagement, presented the young couple with a charming bedroom suite and from Herbert and Willy there was a whole range of kitchen utensils.

Jonathan, not to be outdone, promised, with a wicked twinkle, that they would name their first son after him.

The Captain was horrified.

"Heaven forbid, lad! Have you forgotten my first name is Jonah? But if you have a mind to name him John, I'll be gratified. That is at least my due. Without me this auspicious engagement would not have taken place."

Beth placed a shy kiss on the old sailor's cheek, much to his delight.

Before the Captain finally left, he took Jonathan aside and handed him a handsome gift of money. "I've appreciated your service with me, Jonathan. All those years! I shall miss you sorely," he said gruffly and strode off, setting his hat at a jaunty angle.

Jonathan was visibly touched, watched with Beth, the old man disappear down the street. This gift would go a long way in setting up his surgery.

Mr. and Mrs. Linnett were the first to find a suitable house and moved in thankfully and happily. It had outbuildings where Mr. Linnett could set up his printing machine and was big enough to house his large stock of calico and other material. He was much impressed with the lovely designs used by the African women in their bead-work. Each pattern was a message to the males.

Jonathan and Beth were not quite so fortunate for they required a set of rooms in a house that could be used for a surgery. Until such time, Mr. Linnett suggested, to which the young couple agreed, that the wedding should be postponed for a while, but Jonathan and Beth did meet the Methodist minister to make arrangements for the banns to be called, but no date set.

Eventually, after weeks of house hunting, a property was found. The young couple were thrilled when they were shown over a house, built on Colonial lines, that could be adapted to their needs. There was a large room with an outside door, that would be perfect for a surgery.

"And we'll have chairs out here on this huge verandah, for my patients." Jonathan grinned. "Let's hope there are patients. We'll enclose this part of the verandah with glass."

"And I will hang up curtains," said Beth with housewifely pride. "It is going to be just perfect, dearest."

The rest of the house was also to their taste. With a little love and lots of paint it could become a house of their dreams. The garden too, although overgrown had huge banana clumps and pawpaw trees, flourishing in profusion, much to their delight. Jonathan was already acquainted with these fruits and assured Beth that they would make a tasty fruit salad. There was already, a hand of bananas nearly ripe enough to pick.

They hurried back to the tavern, where Jonathan was still boarding to tell their good news to the Andrews, who promised they would inform their customers and friends about the new surgery. This is what Jonathan had hoped for. When the family were told and the house viewed, they were all impressed, Jed going as far as to offer to carve a name plate, being his contribution to the new venture.

The next event would be Beth's and Jonathan's wedding.

No elaborate preparations for the great day were necessary. It would be a simple affair. Beth would wear her mother's wedding dress and veil, which beyond a little alteration, fitted her perfectly. There would be no guests either, except for the Andrews.

It had been Mr. Linnett's task since their arrival to call in each day to collect any mail that had arrived for them. On the morning of the wedding, he had arrived back with a pleased, satisfied smile and after they had breakfasted, he asked Joanna to deliver a letter for Jonathan which he had picked up at the Receiving Office.

"Don't you think that Beth would be a better postman, Father?" with an arch look at her sister.

"No, no," cried Mrs. Linnett quickly. "There is still packing to do and besides, the groom does not see the bride, until she walks down the aisle."

Joanna obligingly fetched her hat, ramming it on to her head, with not even a glance in the mirror. As she walked down the street, she thought how very pleased her parents were at Jonathan and Beth's marriage. They both simply glowed this morning.

As she approached the house, she was pleased to see several carriages outside the surgery and because she knew Jonathan was busy, she let herself into the house, not noticing that the door should not have been left unlocked.

Joanna walked into the small hallway. After the bright sunlight, the dimness of the room made it impossible to recognise the figure coming out of the drawing-room, until he spoke. "Oh, Jodear!"

"Freddie?" It was just a whisper. "Oh Freddie, you've come," and was swept into his warm embrace as if he would never let her go. They viewed each other for a long moment, not quite believing they were together at last, until he slid his hand through her silky mass of hair to cup her head while he kissed her thoroughly.

For Joanna her topsy turvy world had magically righted itself, but she suddenly drew back her head, her face more radiant, if that were possible, to say, "Freddie, it was you! Oh, I'm so glad!" and threw her arms around his waist. "That makes it absolutely perfect!"

"I say!" exclaimed the disconcerted Mr. Martin, thrown completely off balance. "What on earth — "

"You are the Stranger!" a glow of colour matching her apricot morning gown.

"But — but who is he?" he asked, still bewildered.

"The masked gentleman that night at Father's manufactory. Remember? I — I must admit to a very strong — liking." Her eyes were suddenly shy. "For the first time in my life, I realised I was a woman."

That errant eyebrow of Freddie's rose and with a gentle finger Joanna stroked it back in place. "Only for a little while, Freddie dear, because I then began to miss you so much. I suddenly experienced what loneliness of the spirit meant, that only you could assuage."

This dear girl of his shy? Freddie found this knowledge quite entrancing and his mouth quirked. He had thought he knew every mood of hers, but this aspect of her character, was something new, fragile, dear, his eyes hungrily taking in the softly flushed cheeks. His Jodear was at last aware of him as a man, who loved her dearly.

"You've been my every heart beat," Freddie murmured, leading her into the garden, to a seat under a shady tree. There was so much to discuss.

Joanna was still unsure. "Were you the Stranger, dear Freddie?" He nodded. "But why?"

"Dash it all, dearest! A fellow can't go about helping people openly. Very embarrassing for all concerned. No, much better to do it my way."

She chuckled. "Oh, Freddie! How very romantic of you," her head on his shoulder and sighed. "I'm very glad it was you! I won't now have any guilty feeling."

"I was glad that I could help Uncle Joseph that awful night. Not that it really helped. It did not stop the men smashing all the new machinery later that night."

They were both silent. Remembering. It was Joanna who broke the silence. "Now, dear Freddie, please tell me everything."

He drew her more closely to him and began: "I received a letter from Uncle Joseph, for which I'm eternally grateful, telling me you had — "

"Woken up to the fact that I loved you dearly?"

He nodded. "Mother then went into action, never thought she could. M'father usually does that, but she packed my bags and then my father and I drove madly down to the harbour where, fortunately, there was a steamship preparing to sail to Port Natal that very evening. Your father told me that he had met every ship for weeks, bless him, met me and brought me here.

"Jo dearest, I do like Beth's Jonathan. He has an air of honest manliness that I find most attractive. I'll be proud to call him my brother-in-law. Haven't had much time to talk to him, but what a dreadful journey yours must have been. He has nothing but praise for you and Beth."

"It was Bethie who willingly went down to that dreadful deck where the sick sailors were accommodated." She shuddered, Freddie holding her close.

He lifted her chin with a gentle finger and smiled down at her. "Will you marry me, Jodear?"

"Oh yes, please," she murmured.

"It will have to be today, sweetheart."

"What!" she gasped, sitting up abruptly.

"As your father brought me here, he told me that Beth and Jonathan were to be married this afternoon. Do you think we could make it a double wedding?" Noticing where her thoughts were leading added: "I have a special licence so that will be all right and tight."

"You have to go back, haven't you?" she replied with a loving smile and when he nodded added softly, "I'll go with you."

"Jodear, there is something else I have to tell you, which makes it more imperative that we go back immediately. I mean tonight. I left most of my luggage aboard. The ship sails tomorrow early."

Joanna blinked but could find nothing to say. Her packing — but Freddie went on, "Several days before your letters arrived we learnt from Army Headquarters that Paul had been killed in India. Some skirmish or other."

Aghast, Joanna held his hand against her cheek. "I'm sorry, so very sorry.

253

Poor Uncle Adam and Aunt Fanny! Yes I see. I'll be ready to go aboard with you tonight, dearest."

"Jade Place is waiting for you — "

At that moment Jonathan came out bringing a tray of tea with him. He had a marked twinkle in his eyes.

"Freddie, you surely must have popped the question by now and are sorely in need of some nourishment. A double wedding this afternoon?"

Joanna, suddenly surfacing to more mundane topics, again thought of her packing and what she was going to wear.

"How am I going to manage?" she gasped.

It was Freddie who set her mind at rest. "You are not to worry about a thing, Jodear. Your father said that Aunt Eliza and Nanny would do that for you," passing her a cup of tea which she drank thirstily.

Jonathan, his long legs stretched out comfortably, sipping his tea said with deep feeling, "Jodear, Beth and I will miss you sorely, so will your parents, but I promise you this, Beth and I will look after them." The surgery bell rang and he rose to his feet. "Freddie, I commit this dear girl to you," and strode along the path into the house.

★ ★ ★

Afternoon sunshine filled the small Methodist Chapel, reflecting touches of colour from the stained-glass windows on to the altar as Beth and Joanna, with their father between them, walked slowly down the aisle, Mrs. Linnett wiping away tears. Both girls were radiant, making beautiful brides. Mrs. Andrews had come up trumps, with a loan of her wedding gown for Joanna.

"Dearly beloved — "

"Lord, bless these young couples," prayed Mrs. Linnett, "through joy and sorrow, laughter and tears," giving thanks for her two dear sons-in-law.

The service was over, the organ

poured forth the wedding march and a verse came to Mrs. Linnett.

'Only our love hath no decay,
This no tomorrow hath, nor yesterday.
Running it never runs from us away
But truly keeps his first, last everlasting day.'

Who had written that she wondered. Joseph would know. She must remember to ask him and tucked her hand under his arm feeling his response.

THE END

Other titles in the
Linford Romance Library:

A YOUNG MAN'S FANCY
Nancy Bell

Six people get together for reasons of their own, and the result is one of misunderstanding, suspicion and mounting tension.

THE WISDOM OF LOVE
Janey Blair

Barbie meets Louis and receives flattering proposals, but her reawakened affection for Jonah develops into an overwhelming passion.

MIRAGE IN THE MOONLIGHT
Mandy Brown

En route to an island to be secretary to a multi-millionaire, Heather's stubborn loyalty to her former flatmate plunges her into a grim hazard.

WITH SOMEBODY ELSE
Theresa Charles

Rosamond sets off for Cornwall with Hugo to meet his family, blissfully unaware of the shocks in store for her.

A SUMMER FOR STRANGERS
Claire Hamilton

Because she had lost her job, her flat and she had no money, Tabitha agreed to pose as Adam's future wife although she believed the scheme to be deceitful and cruel.

VILLA OF SINGING WATER
Angela Petron

The disquieting incidents that occurred at the Vatican and the Colosseum did not trouble Jan at first, but then they became increasingly unpleasant and alarming.

DOCTOR NAPIER'S NURSE
Pauline Ash

When cousins Midge and Derry are entered as probationer nurses on the same day but at different hospitals they agree to exchange identities.

A GIRL LIKE JULIE
Louise Ellis

Caroline absolutely adored Hugh Barrington, but then Julie Crane came into their lives. Julie was the kind of girl who attracts men without even trying.

COUNTRY DOCTOR
Paula Lindsay

When Evan Richmond bought a practice in a remote country village he did not realise that a casual encounter would lead to the loss of his heart.

ENCORE
Helga Moray

Craig and Janet realise that their true happiness lies with each other, but it is only under traumatic circumstances that they can be reunited.

NICOLETTE
Ivy Preston

When Grant Alston came back into her life, Nicolette was faced with a dilemma. Should she follow the path of duty or the path of love?

THE GOLDEN PUMA
Margaret Way

Catherine's time was spent looking after her father's Queensland farm. But what life was there without David, who wasn't interested in her?

HOSPITAL BY THE LAKE
Anne Durham

Nurse Marguerite Ingleby was always ready to become personally involved with her patients, to the despair of Brian Field, the Senior Surgical Registrar, who loved her.

VALLEY OF CONFLICT
David Farrell

Isolated in a hostel in the French Alps, Ann Russell sees her fiancé being seduced by a young girl. Then comes the avalanche that imperils their lives.

NURSE'S CHOICE
Peggy Gaddis

A proposal of marriage from the incredibly handsome and wealthy Reagan was enough to upset any girl — and Brooke Martin was no exception.

A DANGEROUS MAN
Anne Goring

Photographer Polly Burton was on safari in Mombasa when she met enigmatic Leon Hammond. But unpredictability was the name of the game where Leon was concerned.

PRECIOUS INHERITANCE
Joan Moules

Karen's new life working for an authoress took her from Sussex to a foreign airstrip and a kidnapping; to a real life adventure as gripping as any in the books she typed.

VISION OF LOVE
Grace Richmond

When Kathy takes over the rundown country kennels she finds Alec Stinton, a local vet, very helpful. But their friendship arouses bitter jealousy and a tragedy seems inevitable.

CRUSADING NURSE
Jane Converse

It was handsome Dr. Corbett who opened Nurse Susan Leighton's eyes and who set her off on a lonely crusade against some powerful enemies and a shattering struggle against the man she loved.

WILD ENCHANTMENT
Christina Green

Rowan's agreeable new boss had a dream of creating a famous perfume using her precious Silverstar, but Rowan's plans were very different.

DESERT ROMANCE
Irene Ord

Sally agrees to take her sister Pam's place as La Chartreuse the dancer, but she finds out there is more to it than dyeing her hair red and looking like her sister.

HEART OF ICE
Marie Sidney

How was January to know that not only would the warmth of the Swiss people thaw out her frozen heart, but that she too would play her part in helping someone to live again?

LUCKY IN LOVE
Margaret Wood

Companion-secretary to wealthy gambler Laura Duxford, who lived in Monaco, seemed to Melanie a fabulous job. Especially as Melanie had already lost her heart to Laura's son, Julian.

NURSE TO PRINCESS JASMINE
Lilian Woodward

Nick's surgeon brother, Tom, performs an operation on an Arabian princess, and she invites Tom, Nick and his fiancé to Omander, where a web of deceit and intrigue closes about them.

THE WAYWARD HEART
Eileen Barry

Disaster-prone Katherine's nickname was "Kate Calamity", but her boss went too far with an outrageous proposal, which because of her latest disaster, she could not refuse.

FOUR WEEKS IN WINTER
Jane Donnelly

Tessa wasn't looking forward to meeting Paul Mellor again — she had made a fool of herself over him once before. But was Orme Jared's solution to her problem likely to be the right one?

SURGERY BY THE SEA
Sheila Douglas

Medical student Meg hadn't really wanted to go and work with a G.P. on the Welsh coast although the job had its compensations. But Owen Roberts was certainly not one of them!

HEAVEN IS HIGH
Anne Hampson

The new heir to the Manor of Marbeck had been found. But it was rather unfortunate that when he arrived unexpectedly he found an uninvited guest, complete with stetson and high boots.

LOVE WILL COME
Sarah Devon

June Baker's boss was not really her idea of her ideal man, but when she went from third typist to boss's secretary overnight she began to change her mind.

ESCAPE TO ROMANCE
Kay Winchester

Oliver and Jean first met on Swale Island. They were both trying to begin their lives afresh, but neither had bargained for complications from the past.